BUBBLE

A TALE OF SOMERSET VILLAGE LIFE

First Published in Great Britain 2017 by Mirador Publishing

Copyright © 2017 by Catherine Holloway
Photographic Copyright © 2017 by Catherine Holloway

All rights reserved. No part of this publication may be reproduced or transmitted, in any form or by any means, without permission of the publishers or author. Excepting brief quotes used in reviews.

First edition: 2017

Any reference to real names and places are purely fictional and are constructs of the author. Any offence the references produce is unintentional and in no way reflects the reality of any locations or people involved.

A copy of this work is available through the British Library.

ISBN: 978-1-911473-86-2

Mirador Publishing
10 Greenbrook Terrace
Taunton
Somerset
TA1 1UT

Bubble

A Tale Of Somerset Village Life

By

Catherine Holloway

Notes for the reader

Welcome to South Somerset! I do hope you enjoy escaping to my countryside retreat. Wrap yourself in the rural bubble of safety and bliss away from the tensions of modern life.

I hope you enjoy my lead character, the ex-popstar who wants to follow the lead of some of his contemporaries in leaving their London "show biz" lives behind and using their fame and or fortune to make a new successful lifestyle in the country.

The book is designed as a light hearted read that allows you to immerse in a world of characters you care about in a setting you love. It also touches on some of the modern strains on rural society and gives a little detail of village life.

Bubble is set in a fictional village in the beautiful hamstone region of South Somerset and captures the beauty of the whole region. You may recognise places you know, though expect enough artistic licence to keep it fictional. The characters are built from my experiences from across the globe and although inspired by Somerset, are not a portrayal of any one person.

I have added a collection of images from my happy moments across the seasons in Somerset (thanks to my family and friends who may recognise some of them.) These are for their uplifting value and not illustrative content. I hope they lift your heart too.

The narrative also contains sneaky reminders from the 1990's, added to capture the spirit of the main character. See what you can spot and find yourself humming!

I am really interested in how the decisions we make are a function of our experiences as well as our character and genetics. In the text, Tamsin has built a safe and controlled life but is unable to truly commit emotionally to her husband. Her background would explain why.

I also believe that no one person is ever entirely to blame for an event, there are many contributing factors that lead up to the final effects of many people's decision making. I try to present this theory through the tangle of interweaving lives and how one person's decision effects the next person's and so forth.

I also feel that most people make poor decisions when they are stressed or unhappy and try to explore this. The less desirable acts of my characters are a result of long term stress or unhappiness. Sometime what may have happened in the distant past and sometime more recently. Their actions are more understandable when they are explored.

I have presented my thoughts in the progress of the characters and I hope that you find it thought provoking.

Read at as much depth as you wish. You may want to take the time to explore these thoughts or you may just want to relax and enjoy the story telling.

Either way I do hope you enjoy.

Dedication

To my beautiful daughter who has been so enthusiastic and creative.
Your ideas are in here!

To my lovely husband for keeping the faith
and my friends who have read and advised.

Preface

1690

The old man stood and stared, wrinkling his eyes as the sun sunk below the steep sided valley that unfurled below him.

As the thin gnarled fingers of pink gripped the darkening sky, he watched the buzzard swoop, with his single cry curling across the valley. The stream that had once refreshed and sustained his people, bubbled noisily across the rocks and towards the plantation they had nurtured, from infancy to high yielding maturity.

Bobtails dashed from view as his eyes progressed into the deep cut that the river had scoured through the slopes. Primroses clung to the banks, standing their ground as the buttercups and forget me nots began to spread and take over their fragile grip of early spring.

All around, lulling his senses was the plaintive grumble of ewes, watching as their lambs high jumped their way around the field and back to their mother's comfort.

"Do it." Were his only words.

Behind him a dark procession of shrouded figures thrust burning torches towards the sky. A low muttering became a louder chanting, over and over until it flooded the soundscape and the buzzard circled and disappeared. The dark capes formed a circle.

"Away with you devil, away with you devil!"

The old man was pushed into the centre of the circle and the chanting became louder and louder, filling his whole being and nauseating his soul.

"Let this troubled village be gone, let the devil leave!"

One shrouded figure placed his hands on the old man's head and then thrust them skyward.

"Leave this man and leave this village!"

The circle opened and the chanting procession led to the wattle and daub thatched cottages that clustered in the lea of the hill. The torches were plunged into the thatches which roared alight in seconds.

"All gone and may it never happen again. This valley must not be used again or the devil himself will arise."

Chapter 1

Gervais James as he liked to be known, (Alex Gervais Jones on his birth certificate, Cock to his school mates), hustled his beautiful blonde model wife Tamsin into the SUV. He took one last look at the luxurious Islington flat that had supported him through the Britpop years, patted his expanding waistline and pulled away into the traffic jam ahead of him. Two hours of stop start London traffic finally got him onto the West Way and heading to South Somerset to the smallholding he had spontaneously purchased by auction.

Life after popstar seemed to be eluding him. Fashion designer and an after-dinner speaker had failed to replicate the income he had made singing humorous jaunty melodies about counter culture in the 90's. Instead of growing old gracefully, enjoying the spoils of a busy youth, he was becoming a flaccid, grey and increasingly penniless version of himself.

Time to change! Gervais decided to put down his heavy black framed glasses and try to do something completely different that would build up his slight frame and his poorly bank balance.

Watching how other celebrities had revived the fortunes of the Cotswolds and Dorset, Gervais was intending to get Channel 4 to bank role his move to South Somerset. They would film the setting up of his small holding, thus raising the house prices in the area so he could sell and finally settle down to drinking his profits in the way he had so successfully snorted the last lot back in 1990's Islington. At this point, even the most obscure channels had rejected his application, stating that they were looking for new ideas and that every inch of interest had been squeezed out of relocation life style TV. Gervais had argued that the reruns of "Location Location Location" still had good viewing figures, but this had not persuaded the good people of TV to take him on.

Sure of his appeal, Gervais had thus invested in a good hand held camera, his smallholding and an SUV and was ready to prove them all wrong – and make some money on the side.

"Down the three oh three to the end of the road!" They hollered to the Levellers track that was famous a few years before Gervais rose to prominence. Before long "Giving me road rage" was rattling around the car as they watched some surprisingly reckless driving. The A303 has had more than its fair share of collisions in the past decade.

Both Tamsin and Gervais managed a long meditative stare at the solemnity of the standing stones near Salisbury as they entered the car park of the A303 where it turns into single lane. "Oh well, they are still trying to decide what to do with this bit." Gervais sighed," An underpass they reckon. Take your free look at the stones while you can!"

"That used to be Sting's house," Gervais uttered a little later, pointing to a chequered house. He was still trying to convince Tamsin that now she was too old for modelling, she could be photographed by "Country Living" in the modern vintage style she would create in the ham stone farmhouse he had acquired.

They finally cruised past the tower on the funny pointy hill and the war memorial on the longer sloping hill. "That's Ham Hill", he stated. "It used to be an Iron Age fort and then it was taken over by the Romans. Since then it has been a quarry for all the beautiful honey stoned houses you can see everywhere." Tamsin smiled at the local knowledge Gervais seemed to have acquired after one trip to the auctioneers. Gervais swung off the A303 and onto some dusty tiny lanes. "Now the SUV will actually be used for what it is meant for!" he chuckled as he bounced Tamsin mercilessly down the rutted grass centred lanes.

"Norton Beauchamp here we are!" He declared as they drove through a cluster of a soft honey coloured cottages. "How are you feeling about your big house in the country?"

He was a little anxious about how his "girl about town" wife would settle into rural domesticity. She had never lived out of London, unless you included extended photo shoot stays in top hotels across the world. Was she made of stern enough stuff to take this new stage of their life? Was he good enough for her to give up London for?

The village was positioned between a group of small funny shaped hills, some pointy and some long and thin with one sharp side and one sloping side. The last of the sun was glinting on the windows and warming the already golden facades. They passed a brown National Trust sign and another for home- made cider.

As they made their way through the lane, the hedges were crammed with tall white flowers made of a myriad of tiny individual blooms. Gateways showed glimpses of sheep and expensive looking horses with their heads down in the grass.

The first houses in the village were the 1930's first red brick council houses with long gardens designed to enable the resident farm labourers to cultivate their own living. Now the gardens were a picture, crammed full of large blousy flowers and neatly clipped lawns. All apart from the one. This was full of old tarpaulins turning green with the moss. Pieces of engine and the detritus of a day's work were scattered across what used to be the lawn.

Popped into gaps, were 1970's houses with long drives and front gardens, where mature trees and ivy had softened the effect of reconstituted stone and large picture windows. Victorian cottages and ancient wonky terraces clustered together as they drew towards the centre of the village. The pub took up the centre of the village, with the enlarged pavement for outdoor merry making and market time. Alongside was an ancient well and water pump. The tall Norman style church tower oversaw it all with the gold weather vane catching the sun. Then the pattern was repeated as they drew to the outer reaches of the other side of the village.

"Jesus Christ!" Gervais swung the SUV off the road and into the hedge. A huge tractor was flying towards him. "How fast can those things go? And look at the size of the bloody thing! The wheels are taller than our whole car!"

The brand-new tractor roared past them at speed with a jolly wave from a blond bobbed, twenty something, at the wheel.

"Now I wasn't expecting that!" Gervais's voice rose with appreciation. "I thought tractors were rusty red, with no roof and an old man at the helm. How much must that cost, and who was she?"

Gervais restarted the car and turned onto a winding lane with grass down the centre. They passed a cluster of converted farm buildings arranged around a square. At the bottom were two huge farm gates. "Your turn, I'm driving" said Gervais with a grin. Ten minutes later when Tamsin had worked out how a gate is opened, Gervais pulled through and stopped on the other side to pick her up. Ahead lay their farm. Manor Farm, Norton Beauchamp.

Tamsin gasped as she finally stepped carefully down from the SUV in her newly acquired wellies of a certain label she had been told was de- rigour in the country.

She hadn't realised Manor Farm was going to be so old. Tiny diamond shaped panes of glass glittered in the evening sun, neatly housed in soft rich gold stone. The thatch had been replaced years ago, with grey slate but the roses that ran wild over the door returned the quaintness of the welcome. She inhaled the sweet smell of hay and rose petals, softer on the nostrils than the thick bitterness of London exhaust. She absorbed the magical ballet of bird song that invaded every sense of her being.

"The area was made rich in the 1700's from the sheep and the rope. The area is particularly fertile and grew good flax, which was spun into rope, and sail cloth to be used on the great voyages to the new world, oh and gloves.

Somerset helped to create the empire!" declared Gervais. "That's why there are lots of these Tudor looking houses. They were farms and made a mint. These side lanes are called droves where the sheep were driven off the moors just to the north there and taken down to be sold in Lyme Regis."

Tamsin smiled at his enthusiasm and hoped that she could embrace the place like he did.

Pushing open the ancient wide oak door with hinges as long as her arm, she entered the cool dark of the hall. Cold flag stone floors greeted her, covered with a rush matting they had been told was made from the trees and reeds from the moor on the other side of the hills. She almost expected a golden retriever to appear snuffling wetly at her ankles, but she had been told this was strictly black lab and springer spaniel country, due to the high incidence of pheasant shooting that seasonally brought people from the city on expensive jaunts to the rain and mud of autumn Somerset.

She stepped inside feeling the delicious cool of the hall wrap around her travel worn body and wandered into the kitchen. Her heart sunk as she registered the shabby 1960's collection of cheap furniture. There were no Victorian dressers that she could refurbish with Farrow and Ball and then show case to the eager journalist as she wrapped her lithe slender body enrobed in "Joules" around them.

Straining her ears, she could hear a faint bubbling like boiling water in the gloomy recess of the corner. Opening the pantry door, she realised that it was furnished with a lively spring that ran from a ham stone bank and into a drain below. "Free refrigeration and ice cold water on tap" she giggled. The spring seemed to chat to her like Suzy, her Grans old budgerigar had when she spent hours waiting to catch a glimpse of her mother.

Gervais thought her family had moved to Spain but in reality, her single mother had relied on prostitution to pay the bills and was more "Fag ash Lil" than the Princess of Monaco that Tamsin alluded to.

Tamsin's conception was a drunken New Year's fumble. That emergency time when everyone feels they need to be with someone – anyone- to start the year on a slightly more positive note. Her father's name was lost in the mists of vodka and cigarette smoke. Her mother had never married and used her femininity, all she had, to make ends meet.

Her brother had been conceived in a similar manner but I suppose you could say the unknown father, this time by pre-paying for his fumble, had contributed a little towards the maintenance of his unknown son.

Fortuitously hanging around the street corners of Poplar had put Tamsin on good terms with gangsters and players who had then introduced her to the right modelling agencies and consequently a catwalk career. Still only in her twenties, Tamsin secured her future by marrying a pop star. He was not the clear-skinned muscular type she dreamed of, but he had a hefty income and a good supply of cocaine. That would do for now. This new foray into the countryside had taken a lot of persuasion, but knowing she was on the wrong side of 30 with a career over and not a financial bone in her body; Tamsin knew what she had to do.

Tamsin's heart began to lighten as she saw the huge ingle nook fireplace. She could see herself curled over Gervais's lap on a lavender sofa with Laura Ashley throw. She thought back to the bespoke kitchens that she had seen in the glossies and knew that she could make this work.

Gervais meanwhile was grunting and scraping in the kitchen. The aga he had coveted when he looked at the place in the auction particulars, was stuck closed with burnt oil and grime. There would be no extra money to live elsewhere whilst they renovated so he had better get it going.

Tamsin meanwhile had climbed the elegant creaking staircase and gasped at the wooden panelled bedroom with tiny windows. She crouched to peer out at the undulating countryside and was immediately taken by the babbling brook that crossed the garden from the valley that spread out before her. She glanced at the plantation to the right and wondered how much of it belong to them. She screwed up her eyes and thought back to the auction particulars. She recalled the decaying barns and the paddocks to the left of the house but not the land immediately to the right. Was it theirs? It had to be, it was so beautiful.

Tamsin felt a warmth on her neck followed by the stinging crunch of Gervais's stubble on her soft skin. She turned and smiled. "Is that ours?" she pointed to the curvaceous land.

"Dunno, it's pretty isn't it. Still either way, we get to look at it!"

Romany's Bubble chattered away as it dropped the summer water down the steep rocky passage it had carved for itself. It sounded happy like that lonely budgerigar chatting to a visitor.

Chapter 2

Helen Withers looked out of the cottage window and over the undulating countryside. She breathed in the fresh morning air and listened to the riot of the dawn chorus.

"Seven more weeks," she murmured. "Seven more weeks until I can relax."

Term had taken its toll on Helen. Working in a small town primary school was tough. Underfunded by the state and ignored by the researchers, Briary Gates had more than its fair share of troubled children.

Some had escaped from their ex-Soviet Union homes into the new European Community, with no English and a mind filled with the horrors they had experienced. Others were dragged with a myriad of siblings out of their chaotic family homes, unfed and unwashed into school.

New research on how to tackle these situations was still the premise of the inner city highly funded school whilst the small towns were left to fight for themselves whilst the rural school funding was cut and cut again.

Helen was drained by the violence, unruliness, and additional paperwork expectations. The new curriculum raised the expected outcomes by a year so her struggling, empty bellied, children would fall yet further behind.

Schools had to spend time and money that was in short supply to decide their own curriculum and how to assess it and then ensure it matched other schools and was achievable in the time given. It didn't help that the school was on notice to improve with OFSTED imminent.

The future looked grey, monotonous unachievable. Up at six to get in before eight and home at six to carry on with the paperwork was proving unsustainable. Helen felt like a Middle Eastern donkey having additional loads added and whipped by performance meetings to keep going.

"What would you do Mum?" Helen often muttered to herself. Sometimes in her dreams, her parents would visit her and talk softly and reassuringly to her. She used to feel the warmth of their love soften the strain in her muscles and heart. She would finally feel safe and loved.

The 6 am alarm would then go off and Helen was violently returned to the cold harsh reality of life at the present. She often woke with tearstains on her face.

Helen had been left the family home, when her parents had died together on a volunteering mission to Africa. Spurred on by the desperation that pushed itself into their lives at 6pm every evening on both major channels, they had packed up and gone to help in any way they could. Their 4wd had hit one of the many potholes and turned over killing them both outright. Helen was left alone with a crumbling cottage, an unpaid mortgage, and a desperate need for guidance.

Covering the stress related dermatitis on her face, with layers of concealer; Helen grimaced and was out of the house by ten to seven.

Helen was due to be observed today, she was worn out and had little left to give. Pulling up to school, a huge wave of nausea came over her. "Enough" said a voice inside her.

Helen wasn't sure whether it was her mother speaking, or even if she had uttered it aloud. She envisaged the Head with a clipboard and frown entering her room and flicking through her books. Her stomach wobbled and her voice rose to a squeak. Her head began to fill with a strange detached muffled feeling and her eyes lost focus.

Before she knew it, Helen was back in her car and home. Pacing up and down and shaking, she stood up and sat down; she stood up and sat down again. Her hands trembled. A boiling sensation bubbled up within her and she ran to the toilet and vomited.

Helen couldn't settle, she needed to talk, but to who? Her parents were gone, her neighbours were on a cruise and Jane was in the shop working. She felt the need to talk to someone and get things resolved.

She couldn't sit still until she had done something.

She still hadn't rung in sick. What would she say? She couldn't pick up the phone.

She put her head in her hands and said over and over between tears "Mum, mum, mum."

Eventually Shaking with fear, she texted the school and told them she had been sick and would be off for a few days. Then she phoned the NUT for advice. "Don't worry, we will sort it." Go to the Doctor and get signed off, you need it.

The receptionists declared the doctor had no appointments until next Friday.

Persisting, because she didn't really know what else to do, Helen's tears and anguish finally got her a telephone appointment.

The Doctor who was getting very used to signing teachers off on stress, booked her onto the waiting list for talking therapies and printed a prescription and a sick note. She would have to come in and pick them up then find a way of emailing it to the school. The local library would probably help her to scan and email it.

Helen now felt able to complete the task, go home and drink herself into sleep. The "Six O'clock News" droned on about more ISIS, war, refugee crisis and world depravation as she slumped on the sofa.

Chapter 3

"Bloody Arse!"

Tamsin heard a shout from below. Her heart shot into her throat. Gervais was not known for his DIY skills and she wasn't enamoured by the idea of a trip to A and E!

Rushing downstairs to see what Gervais had done, she saw him holding a battered camera.

"I forgot we are supposed to film every step of our journey. I went to the car to get the camera and it fell out of the boot! Look at the state of this!" Tamsin supressed a giggle as Gervais held up the camera, now with shattered lens. "Where's my bloody phone? It'll have to do instead!"

For the next hour, they filmed take after take to ensure that they look suitably attractive in a travel worn manner as they pretended to set eyes on the house for the first time.

Tamsin was in her element and orchestrated some beautiful poses. She was good at making things look happy, not so good at really making the feelings come alive in herself.

It was drawing dark before Tamsin suggested they unpacked the car and sorted something temporary for the evening.

The removals were coming first thing in the morning, so they would need to sort the airbeds and sleeping bags now.

"To the future!" they clinked prosecco glasses together and collapsed in an exhausted heap.

The following morning, they awoke to a thumping at the door. "The removals men aren't due until at least 10am," muttered Gervais. "It is barely the crack of dawn!"

He ran downstairs and was greeted by a violent thump to his shoulders that winded him and knocked him backwards.

"Down Aga! What have I said about greeting people like that! Wake up it's a beautiful morning! Most awfully sorry, just wanted to greet you into the neighbourhood. Captain Phelps, pleased to meet you, I live in the barn conversion just down the road. How are you finding things?"

Gervais both recoiled and recovered to view a greying moustachioed man dressed head to toe in green carrying a rather large weapon and a bouncing black Labrador with a tail that whipped his legs with increasingly annoying ferocity.

"Just off to try my hand at a few bunnies wondered if you wanted to join me."

Gervais explained the removals situation and arranged a date at the pub in the evening. "See you anon!" Shouted the retreating figure as he set off towards the valley at a rapid pace a black furry rocket zig zagging across his path.

That evening Tamsin and Gervais giggled as they wandered down their bumpy lane to the local pub.

"I didn't know people like that still existed! Do you think it is a publicity stunt to get us to go to the pub? I must make sure I film some of it, he really is a hoot! I wonder what else we will meet when we get down with the common people!

"God I ache – I thought we paid a mint for the removal men to do all that work. Why do I hurt so much? And we've hardly made a dent on it. I still haven't opened my awards box. Where will I put all my Brits?"

Captain Phelps, or Steve as he tried to prevent people from knowing, had been retired from the TA after the first Gulf War, where he sustained injury to his ears and to his pride. Still determined to play the military man, he had secured work as a local gamekeeper and had managed to keep up the pretence of the military hero, claiming the work as a "distraction" rather than the necessity that it really was.

Country Gent was his aim and he was determined to get the newbies on side before anyone else could get to them to destroy the myth. He had portrayed this image for so long that he had begun to believe the heroic end to his career that he had invented for himself and forgotten the sink estate from the wrong end of town and the public swimming pool attendant career he had started out with. He would be horrified to think that anyone would discover his guilty past. He shuddered when he drove past his previous existence in Taunton. The filth of his parent's alcohol ravaged lifestyle had made his skin crawl and so now his house was modern, spotless and every part of his life was impeccable.

Unfortunately, he lived in an area with many helicopter pilots and naval engineers due to the local Yeovilton Navy base and international helicopter manufacturer and they took his story with a pinch of salt. Steve was humoured to his face but behind his back, he was thought of merely as humorous.

With all due respect, he was successful in his work and should have been content with his military success and gamekeeper career. The middle-class pretentions making more of a point of humour than "one of the boys" with the locals. The "Captain Mainwaring" look was far less appealing than "Poor boy done good." If only he could see that.

Finally twiddling the ends of his moustache and popping his ears to relive the post war tinnitus, he gave a short whistle and set off to the pub in his tweeds with Aga his black lab twirling around his ankles.

Gervais peered at the door of 'The Coachman's Arms.'
"Doesn't look very welcoming. Stinks of old beer." Gervais twisted the circular handle with a stiff clunk and pushed forwards the door.
"Reminds me of the old pubs my Mum used to frequent," muttered Tamsin, biting her lip quickly before she gave away any more of her less than savoury past.
"What's that?" Before Tamsin could think of a damage limitation response, another black lab greeted them. This one was fatter, older and suffered from halitosis. As they squinted into the dark recess of the pub, they were met with a dark abyss. The interior was still painted in dark colours with

one of those madly patterned carpets that you can vomit on without anyone being any the wiser. The dog wandered off scraping its bottom along the carpet as it went.

Tamsin looked down at her new white strappy sandals in dismay. She had refrained from stilettoes and moved to wedges to be a little more country, but now she knew her green wellies were probably more suitable.

Tamsin was always keen to fit in with the crowd, or rather be the most beautiful and stylish member of the crowd. As a child, she had stuck out like a sore thumb, tall, painfully thin and unwashed. Tamsin rarely saw her mother because she would be out on the game, trying to feed her children in the only way she knew.

Tamsin's younger brother had been her only friend. They had brought each other up and Tamsin had tried to keep this up when she was modelling around the world. When she was away, he began to use heroin to fill the void of missing motherly love.

Once on her return, he had disappeared and had finally been found overdosed, curled up in the foetal position in a disused flat in Willesden.

Tamsin used both her career and men to gain mental and penury comfort. She wrapped herself, not in love for she was not sure what that looked like, but in mental comfort of having all the things she should have achieved – a famous rich husband, a good career and a superb figure draped in the latest fashions. If she shone, no one could criticise her ever again and she would never have to go back to Poplar and beg for attention from her mother.

Dragging herself back to the job in hand, Tamsin walked into the dark room. Closer to the bar, the carpet had acquired that shiny black layer that stilettos would have sunk into and collected the black detritus around the heel and carried it home. Tamsin hung back, stepping sideways carefully.

"Evening" came a voice from behind a curtain of dusty pewter and dimpled glass drinking vessels. A plain man appeared. Plain in every way. Slightly overweight, but not huge, greying black greasy hair in no particular style and clothes that covered but didn't enhance his appearance. A face, neither ugly nor attractive, about 50 ish.

"I be John, pleased to meet you. Aren't you the pop staaars from London taken on Old Tom's place?"

Gervais physically grew a centimetre at the description. However, he would prefer the term "rocker" to "pop star."

"Gervais pleased to meet you, this is my wife Tamsin." Tamsin giggled and gave a girlish wave in the hopes that this would avoid having to press the flesh with those heavy paws.

"What do you recommend I try?" Gervais smiled, discreetly pressing record on his phone.

"Is you a bidder maan or a cyeder man?" Responded John in the slow drawl, elongating and widening his vowels in the Somerset way. Gervais looked at the selection of lager on offer and opted for the draft cider. Tasting the commercial sweet concoction, he was genuinely pleased and wondered why he had never gone for it whilst in London. It was certainly available, but he had never tried anything more than strong designer lagers or Belgium Beers from that fashionable pub in Broadway Market.

"Aand for the laedy….?" Tamsin looked at the array in front of her and not trusting the wine, opted for a gin and slim line. Lime was not forthcoming.

"Toodle doo!" In marched Captain Phelps. "How are you settling in? Good day with the removals?" "Toodle doo" was as close as Steve dared get to declaring "Tally Ho!" knowing that would be verging on the ridiculous.

"How's the other half today?"

John sub consciously put his hand up to his cheek that was beginning to feel tender already. "Lovely!" he responded "Just puddin on 'er war paint"

Aga landed on the carpet with a thump, grunted and closed her eyes.

"Comes here often does he?" Gervais remarked.

"Ah that dog do know the place as well as my Pam do." John replied.

Tamsin wondered if Pam was the "other half" or the rotund black lab that was alarmingly close to her new white wedges.

They sat in the window, Tamsin opted for the hard-wooden chair as the bunk cushions on the window seat looked like they may stain her white jeans.

"Who owns that valley by the river?" Tamsin asked. "I can see it from the house and it is beautiful"

"You do!" said Captain Phelps "But don't get excited, there is a covenant on that land passed down since the beginning of time. Old Tom's family have always owned that land as far back as anyone can remember. It must not even be dug up or have veg grown on it. Not even in the war did they touch that. All you can do is graze sheep on it. Not even horses as their big heavy hooves break up the land.

Waste of space if you ask me. The gypsies always stop on it when they go and harvest the Martock beans, but even they don't do more than graze. Think that might be where it gets its name, the river I mean, Romany's Bubble.

Bubble for the river, Bubble of their dreams, Bubble for a protective place where no one and no nasty thoughts can harm you. For many in the village the bubble served a range of needs.

I have been wanting to game keep on it for years but Old Tom wouldn't let me, or at least use it to graze my horse but no. Witch craft they used to say. Been a few years now though and now Old Tom, the last of the family has passed, I suppose it is worth a try."

Unwittingly, Captain Phelps has just set up a spiral of events that would be the cause of much change and much excitement throughout the village. Some of it would have a positive effect, but for some, the ramifications would be much deeper.

Chapter 4

Helen stood looking out of her bedroom window at the beautiful valley below. It had been 3 weeks since she had been signed off work and she had not yet left the house. Her face was still grey and her hair mousy and lank. Pootle the chocolate poodle was fed up with the garden and had dropped into her own depression. Helen just wanted to hide from view. She didn't want to think about real life, not to walk the dog, pay the milkman or anything. She had begun to talk to her mother and father more regularly now. She would ask them what she should do, from the future of her life to whether she should open a tin of baked beans or not.

The house, however was immaculate, she used her stressed energy to create some order in her life. Her career may be careering out of control, but here was something she could maintain. It was somehow soothing, cathartic to put her house in order, even if she could not extend it to the analogous meaning. She would show off to her parents what she had achieved.

"Look Dad, I mended that creaky floorboard. It won't bother us anymore."

She sighed as the sun set, lazily stretching stripes of magenta over the valley and throwing flashes of light beams from distant reflections. The blackbird scolded at Pootle in the garden, fluttering his wings, outraged that the peace had been broken. The buzzard continued to soar above the valley making its empty cry. The stream continued its happy chuckle and Helen felt solace in its happiness. At least the world was continuing, even if she was not ready to be part of it.

In the distance, she could see movements at Manor Farm. Helen lazily wondered what the new owners would be like. The farm was slowly crumbling since Old Tom had died and she wondered who had the money to take it on. Unlikely to be locals, probably someone selling their London, two bed apartments for the price of a mansion in Somerset. The fields were still empty but she could see the windows reflecting flashes of light at they were opened.

She heard the clatter of metal on tarmac and looked out of her tiny cottage window to see Captain Phelps trotting sideways down the road on his big bay hunter.

"Guess Betsy is needing a little more work," mused Helen. Having being a pony club rider as a child, she knew about that deep stomach churn that inflicted you when your horse was repeatedly doing what he wants to at speed and ignoring your requests to stop. She tried to glance at the bit he was using, but couldn't make it out in the speed he was past.

Helen had known Phelps since he came to the village as a veteran in the 90's. Although she found his 1920's upper class accent rather amusing, she grudgingly enjoyed his conversation when she met him on walks and in the pub. He had taught her about game keeping and how to hold a shotgun after her parents had passed away. Phelps and his wife had been her saviours and helped her throughout the darkest of hours. She wished him well.

Gervais was about to become a livestock owner. He knew what to do, he had read all about it on the internet.

The chickens were easy; he went to the local rehoming centre for battery hens for £5 each. He had filmed it all, grabbing the poor featherless, miserable broods and tucking them into the cage to drive home in the boot of the SUV.

Gervais had been brought to tears, when he had released them into their extensive coop. It was like they did not know what to do with themselves. At first, the girls had hidden in the house and had not wanted to come out. When they finally began to timidly venture into their newfound freedom and realised how much space they had, they had begun to scatter about pecking wildly. It had taken all Gervais and Tamsin's energy to get them back into the house at nightfall.

Feeling good about their endeavours, and newly educated, they decided to go for old-fashioned rare breed sheep. Raise them organically, send them off for use in historical films and sell the wool and organic local lamb. Hopefully one of the local countryside TV shows would be interested in the story. Valuable publicity for his "Rent a Ram" project.

Tamsin in the meantime was beginning to realise that country living was not completely a decade in the past. Expecting little from the Pilates and High Intensity Interval Training classes, she had rocked on up to the 1940's village hall on a tummy full of pasta and wine and had been rather taken by surprise. On arrival, she had been pleased to note how many people there were in the village under 30 and was surprised they were all lining up for something as sedate as Pilates. Sarah the instructor was trained in London and kept herself up to date by returning for city jaunts under the guise of professional development. Sarah was not one to let anyone take a breath!

Two hours later, there was not one part of Tamsin's body that had not been stretched, strained, and worked to the max. "Did you enjoy it?" Asked Sarah. Tamsin could hardly limp home, but was pleased with how friendly and normal everyone had seen. "Coming to the pub on Tuesday evening? Girl's night out. We get out the skittles, get out the wine, and have a blast. By the way John in the pub might look a bit spit and sawdust but he will order you in a crate of what you fancy." Tamsin noted that with a grin and was determined to join in and get to know everybody.

The pub was great, the girls were great and Tamsin had learned to wear leggings and boots, rather than white jeans and wedges. They screeched their way through hurling the heavy misshapen wooden skittle ball at the old wooden pins and hollered as it sent them flying across the room. It was a bit like bowling but without the silly shoes and the health and safety.

"The new posh pubs have sunk the skittle alley so that you can raise or lower it and use the room as a function room. Very clever it is." Sarah explained. "We love this place because it may be shabby but it is a proper boozer. Whatever happens in the "Arms" stays in the "Arms". Everyone drinks hard and everyone forgives and forgets. Cigarettes and alcohol, that's this place, we may just be a village but we don't thrive on gossip, well not that much anyway. Watch out for Willy though, he has a mouth on him."

"Willy?" questioned Tamsin.

"Well it is never *won't* he!" Guffawed Sarah "Willy is known for his willingness and his rather overactive willy" How his parents knew what to call him at such a young age I don't know." He is the local odd job man. Do your garden, fix your shelves, build a barbeque, you name it, but on the way, he picks up all the gossip and some of the house wives too! Tell your Gervais to bolt the doors; he will be after a looker like you!"

Tamsin giggled, she was beginning to really love village life and she could do with a "hotty" like Willy to do the garden. She was going to get him involved super- fast. Gervais was rather thin in the arm and round in the belly. Not that she wanted any willy, just a fit body doing the garden and all the village gossip. What more could a girl want?

Tamsin had never been a great ambassador for love and sex, to her; it had always been her currency, a passport to a better life. Deep feelings had eluded her over the years and she couldn't be bothered to seek it out on a purely recreational level. She certainly wasn't going to risk her home and life for it. However, everyone needed a "diet coke" moment.

Perhaps she should invite some of her friends to join her. She scanned her mind for possibilities, weren't thick on the ground. Her circles in 90's London had been more about being seen in the right place at the right time, rather than forging strong relationships. Not having the role model from her mother on how to do this, Tamsin had wanted that security, but didn't know how to achieve it, or what it looked like when offered to her. She relied on her looks and men for her security. She wondered if this could be a new beginning.

Gervais in the meantime had the deeds out to his new purchase. Sure enough, the boundary of his land seemed to include the valley and woodland. It would be a bind if he had to maintain it and not use it. He could envisage four executive homes with large gardens and front drives big enough to hold five range rovers each.

Livestock he was finding a bind. The chickens were ok; they were fenced in from the fox and had an automatic feeder and night-time doors. He was having more trouble with the specialist sheep he had purchased. Nobody had taken up his offer of help and he ended up going to the big auction ground off the M5 and keeping his fingers crossed for the quality and value for money of his purchase. Thank God, for the internet, which had kept, him informed of suitable prices, breeding and availability. He made a haphazard attempt at raising his hand at the correct time, managed to end up with a new flock of pregnant stock, and hoped to enlarge his flock quickly. They seemed to eat through the grass, make serious amounts of noise and didn't seem to be making any bookings.

He was a little worried about Tamsin. She seemed to have met a good crowd and seemed to be spending less and less time at home. She was quite happy to spend money on the new bespoke kitchen at £12k and kitting out each room with extremely expensive vintage paint. She seemed to have found all the independent designer retailers and yet not discovered Clarks Designer Outlet village in Street. He was haemorrhaging money and yet did not seem to be bringing any in. He needed Tamsin to start talking to the female glossies. He had sent some of his footage to Ch. 4 and Endemol and had little response. Gervais took off his heavy black glasses, rubbed his eyes and ran his hand through his greying but expensively cut hair.

What he needed was a good scandal, that would get the papers interested. His thoughts wandered back to the covenant on the land, was there any mileage in that? Was it worth a go?

Chapter 5

Jake Isaacs held his head in his hands. Where could they go now? They had been living on a disused bit of land on the side of the main road since they had been thrown off their old land for flouting building regs. Now the council had caught up with them and served an eviction notice. Could it wait and go to court, biding them some time to find somewhere? Absent minded, he rumpled 'Enry the lurcher hound's coat and sighed. This was no life, not for him, not for his old Dad Eli, or Ellie and the kids.

Phelps was eating breakfast at 7am with his wife Jane. She was getting ready to open the shop in half an hour and he was about to go and check his fencing and young birds. Jane was solid, caring, dependable, if a little plain. She put up with Phelps and looked up to the ex-military man that she had married. She liked her life in a barn conversion, living in a beautiful local community. She knew everyone, had a good social life and lots of firm friends. Her husband, if not demonstrative was kind.

He kept her awake with wild dreams, yelling or coughing or thinking he couldn't breathe. Quite often, she had woken to a smack in the mouth, but she loved and respected Steve Phelps and so didn't say a word.

They had both decided that they did not want children. Phelps felt he was too damaged after the war to be able to look after one. Jane resigned herself to the same after years without contraception had not born fruit. She had her dog, her garden and the Shetland pony. She was not so keen on Steve's hunter and wished he would go for an old cob, but that was not Steve's way.

They were discussing Helen. Both had a soft spot for her since her parents had died, leaving her in the lurch with a smelly needy dog and a mortgage to pay. They had both taken her under their wing, Jane offering love and hugs, Steve taking her out riding and walking to get her out of herself and teach her a love of the countryside. He enjoyed her company, a bit like having a little sister. It made him feel he was doing something right. She was good with the horses too, helping to educate him with her pony club knowledge.

Both realised something was wrong. The car was not leaving the house, the dog was not walked and the front drive did not have a weed in it. Knowing Helen, they both decided time was needed and so apart from delivering the post and the parish magazine through the door with a sneaky glimpse in the house, they decided not to trouble her.

Tamsin meanwhile had been back up to London to get her hair highlighted. She had explained to Gervais that this was a specialist job that needed doing by people who knew her hair. Unconvinced Gervais had made her promise to go back to her agency and to one of the Red Top papers to see if she could sell their story. "You still look fit, put on a tight pair of Jodhpurs and a low-cut top if that is what it takes." She managed to pick up the hope of an anti- aging cream contract if she kept her face out of the sun and had a derma-abrasion. She was also told to get the house sorted before she could expect even a 2-page spread in the glossies. Feeling rather despondent Tamsin spent the rest of her money consoling herself with Cristal Champagne at the hotel bar, slurring her misery to the bar tender, who was too young to recognise her.

Helen decided it was time to take her first steps beyond the garden gate. She waited until dusk and the owls were beginning to call before she started. She knew what she was going to say if anyone asked and she was ready. Hearing the familiar ring of horseshoes on the road, she ducked back and watched Captain Phelps ride past on Betsy, his hunter. She nodded and ducked her head so he would not try to make contact. He was the last person she wanted to tell about her quickly diminishing career. She felt so stupid for having failed, for giving up, for not being able to do it. How can you explain that to people?

"Oh yes, I am so rubbish that I can't do my job any more. In fact, I am so rubbish that instead of handing in my notice, I ran off like a sissy and was sick. By the way, did I tell you I take drugs to keep me normal?" Nausea rose in her throat and she turned to dive into the sanctuary of her house again.

Pootle leapt around her legs and dashed zigzagging around the road with her nose firmly down and her stubby tail up. He ran back, licked Helen's hand, and then ran off again. Never being one for cruelty to animals. Helen bit her lip and proceeded.

Hopping over the gate, Helen took the path along the stream and through the fir plantation. She loved listening to the rich sound of the birds in the forest. It was so dense that it was magical. She had tried a meditation cd that had been recommended by her doctor, but realised that the bird singing on that was not a patch on the real world.

She sighed contentedly. "I just have to sort out the end of this career and start another…."

As she passed out of the forest and onto the hilltops, she could hear the beautiful complex burble of a late lark. It was so beautiful and peaceful; no wonder Vaughn Williams had written a whole piece of music about it. She followed the narrow path and gazed down to the moors ahead of her. Being on the top of the last hill before the levels, meant that you could see for miles. It was exciting in the winter to see the shimmer of the flood land and then, in the other direction, the Quantocks and Blackdowns covered in snow.

As she descended, she could hear the comforting, sniffly, cropping of grass. Two horses were head to the ground in the field. The thoroughbred was on full grass stuffing away and still as slim as a greyhound. Meanwhile penned in to a threadbare inch of land was a Shetland, belly like a barrel. Helen sighed; she was more like a Shetland, constantly having to refuse food to keep a half-decent body. Her thoughts wandered to the new thoroughbred of the village, Tamsin, wasn't it? Bet she ate like a horse and looked like a greyhound with no effort. Still popstar husband or not, Helen preferred a little more muscle and a little less belly on her men. Not that she had one, working twenty-four – seven had put pay to that.

She had been watching the progress of Old Tom's land, they had bought chickens which Helen appreciated, she loved the sound of the morning cockerel, she was used to getting up at the same time as it, unlike the Hamptons next door who preferred to party late and rise late too. The sheep were unlike any others she had seen. She had researched them on the internet, found them to be black Welsh Mountain, and made a good price at market because they are hardy and can be crossbred well. They looked a little bit like Dexter cows from a distance. She wondered whether they would get into horses. This tended to be lucrative in Somerset. People seemed to have back into horses in the last few years, especially piebald gypsy cobbs. She was tempted to revive her knowledge, but 9 hours at school followed by work in the evening made it unviable.

She looped back towards her house, drinking in the last of the cool air and hearing the cackle of an owl, she swept inside feeling better than she had in days.

"Now, onto the Union to find out what I need to do next!" Helen thought. She was feeling a little more inspired and a little less useless than she had in the last few weeks.

John was beginning to serve in the pub. He was exhausted. Last night his wife Clara had gone through three bottles of wine on her own. He wouldn't mind her drinking the profits but she would get so angry and then she was violent. He knew this wasn't the life for her, early mornings and late nights but she could be more civil about it, or get a different job and let him hire someone more amenable for the bar. Then perhaps he wouldn't have to cover up the bruises.

He felt such a drip, running a failing pub, the bills coming in thick and fast and feeling alone and helpless. He knew the place looked bad; it needed a woman's touch.

"Evening, Captain, how's that beautiful horse of yours? I saw you riding past earlier, 'er's looking good." John mustered up his best welcoming beam.

"Usual?" He poured Steve Phelps a Butcombe Ale, the name guaranteed to make any visitors giggle.

"Yes, she is rather fresh at the moment" Phelps replied. "She took me for rather a blast over the bridle path. I was hanging on for dear life, thank goodness, a walker didn't come the other way, it could have got rather messy! I had better get her out more, or enrol one of the village youngsters to keep her schooled for me."

John smiled, wishing a youngster might school his wife, that would keep her drink and anger fuelled hands off his face. He dismissed the "getting her out more"

"How's the missus?" Steve's wife Jane was meek and would never question her husband. He had chosen well. She worked in the local shop, recently converted to a co-op at the fury of older locals. The unsold stock generated a regular supply of bread and vegetables at their sell by date, which supplemented their income well. Steve was known to go lamping himself to startle the rabbits and bring home some supper. Maintaining the environment for his game would be the response if anyone questioned it, not that anyone ever had.

"Has that new filly Tamsin been in recently?" Steve changed the subject, "Jolly nice I think, pert bottom, not been squashed in a saddle I bet!" John laughed knowing it was more than his job and his face was worth to comment. They discussed the females skittle game and resulting drunken laughter.

"Women do make a terrible noise when they have been on the sherbet, don't they? Still at least they don't end in fisty cuffs."

John wasn't so sure about that.

"Saw our Helen out earlier too. Haven't seen her for a while, didn't look like she wanted to talk, so I pushed Betsy on and let her pass. Haven't seen her going out to work for a while either, car seems to always be in the drive. Perhaps I should get Jane to pop over and see her? Check she is ok? Might get some gossip on Tamsin and her pop star. Helen's house over looks their land, doesn't it?"

"I no 'iced them Isaacs are baack in the paper again," John drawled. "Got int trouble with the buildin' regs, silly fool. Still what 'arm is there in buildin' himself a toilet, bedder than 'aving it all over ee's field I reckon."

"Wonder where they will go now? It's no life for the kids, just got them settled and doing well in school and now they will have to be off again. It is just perpetuating the cycle. No steady education, no chance of a decent job and making a living. They keep all their vans and trailers quiet behind the hedge, what's the problem? They never give me any trouble."

"Well, they 'ave been offered council 'ouses but the locals don't make 'em welcome. Do all sorts like break the doors and park stuff over the gateway. Think they are gunna rob 'em and trash the place wiv their broken cars. I thinks they should be allowed to 'ave their own land back and do what they like to it."

"But there again, I couldn't put windows in the back of my house because it had to look like a barn. Bloody planners. Why should the gyppos be able to do what they like on their land when I can't do it to mine? If it was fair, I wouldn't mind. And how much tax do they pay? They just seem to buy and sell, breed ponies and do all the seasonal farm work – along with the Poles. Fair's fair, they shouldn't be pestered the way they are, it is racism and fear, but then if they paid their way, people might be a little more reasonable. Any way Somerset are good to the gypsies, there are plenty of well- kept sites they could go to."

"Pr'aps they should save up and buy land and then use it nicely, like them hippies over near 'am 'ill. Them's don't cause no bother an' ever one knows 'bout them and their lush apple juice them sells. Still, I don' know about whaaat they do and whaat they don' pay to be 'onest . But I do know thic problem aint going away. But I'll tell 'ee this, they would be welcome in 'ere if they spends their money like everyone else."

"Cheers"!

"Are you ever going to get that mutt wormed? It doesn't make this pub very welcoming you know, fat old dog scratching her arse on the carpet."

"You talking 'bout mye wife again?"

Chapter 6

"Woohooo!" Tamsin clattered down the oak stairs. "We got a gig, we got a gig!" She leapt on Gervais who swung her round, putting her down quickly as his arms began to shake. "Country Sights want to come and interview us! They want to see our kitchen and your photographs and how we are settling in with the sheep. Whoop whoop! we did it! Oh yes, we did it! Fame and money here we come! Right they are due in 5 days, time to build up those muscles of yours and time to clean and organise!"

Manor Farm was a hive of activity over the next few days. Sheep were cleaned, grass cut, chickens spruced and extra eggs laid in their boxes to make it look like the hens were laying well. Fences were creosoted leaving a warm country smell across the yard. Inside the walls were "Farrow and Balled" and the old kitchen table found in an antique shop was scrubbed.

Gervais decided a wild night at the pub was due, so he could get in some loving and boost that glow on Tamsin's face. Pregnancy had not been an option whilst she was modelling, but that could be the news to boost their magazine article career!

They walked up to the pub bedecked in new jeans (not white) and trainers. Tamsin had curled her straight hair and looked stunning. Gervais grinned, his muscles had begun to grow and he hoped to show them off later.

"Oh God, no..."

Pam was sitting on the bench next to the bar and was lapping up the stale beer in the drinks tray.

"I hope you are planning on putting that through the glass washer before I get to use it."

"Glaass waasher? That aint worked for years! Now what can I get you today lovely people. Your own Chablis Tamsin? What about you Gervais, got some new local guest ales on, and I have bought in some San Miguel for you trendy types."

"Lovely!" They both giggled and held up their own glasses that they had learned to bring from home.

"You can keep them 'ere you know like ever one else do." John pointed to the hanging glasses. Tamsin and Gervais failed to respond.

"Saw the Captain belting past on that monster of his earlier. Pretty lively, isn't it? Are we going to see the helicopter air lift him from a field soon?" Gervais smiled.

"Aye she is a bit wild that one. He is a brave man I think."

"Mornin' all!" In came an expensively dressed man of about 40 with a dark curvy wife on his arm. "You must be the pop stars. Enjoying the peace and quiet? Tom and Estella Wesley, pleased to meet you. What are you both having? Aha learned quickly, got your own in! How are you settling in to Old Tom's place? Lovely bit of land. House needs a bit of work, but I've seen a few white vans around the place, what have you been up to?"

Tamsin and Estella settled down to chat about kitchens, local flooring and oak furniture whilst Tom and Gervais learned a bit more about how each made their fortunes in the '90's.

Tom built an internet site that he later sold on and invested the money into property. He was a happy man who didn't need to work and spent his time renovating local properties that took his interest. South Somerset was a little gem because the housing and local areas were stunning and rising all the time. Some areas were banned from development but with the shortage of houses and local government requirements to provide local affordable housing, new brownfield sites were being found all the time. People were selling off their old orchards and creating new-gated housing complexes with twenty highly finished houses with gardens the size of a baby's sock. One bungalow with sloping lawns had created a set of three new build four bedroom, three story houses.

Great if you don't mind parking on the narrow lane and don't want to lie down in your garden. Just don't try to swing a cat!

Gervais began to cook up his ideas.

"Toodle do!" A heavy weight slammed down in the seat next to Tamsin. How's life in the countryside going? Missing the availability of take-away at two am yet?

Tamsin laughed, "Hi, Captain Phelps. No, I stick to good old toast and marmite after a night on the lash, and of course fresh eggs from our new hens. I am actually loving it here, I reckon in my previous life I must have been a farmer."

"Not in those fashion wellies I keep seeing you in. Time to get a pair of these! Steve's feet were encased in beautiful leather and suede knee-high boots. "All weather, comfy as you like, waterproof and they breathe. Everyone has them around here, they work a treat. They tend to come up cheap on the stalls of the country shows as surplus stock; otherwise, you can pay £200 for them. Look pretty good with those long legs and tight arse of yours. Not that I have been looking of course."

Tamsin giggled politely and wondered if men really were the same all over the world.

At that, moment the conversation was mercifully halted as the door was flung open, hitting the wall behind it.

"Here come the beautiful ones!" muttered John.

"Hey hey hey everyone, here we are!" In walked a bunch of young fit lads with a huge variety of hair- cuts, from shaved all over, to large pampered Essex quiffs, to blonde dreadlocks crashed through the door. "Meet the local football team".

Tamsin was amused to find that there was no rugby team as that was hard work which would get in the way of drinking and young farmers do's. But the locals were good at kicking around a ball and were at the lead of the local pub league. A day of ground working and farming kept these boys fit enough to enjoy life to the full. And they did.

After a round of vodka red bulls and Jägermeister shots, the noise level increased and the boys had everyone joining in. Before Gervais knew it, their attention had turned to him and they began singing one of his old anthems. Parks, parachutes, big houses and clean teeth and being caught by the fuzz crashed around the pub in tuneless cacophony.

Everyone was laughing and drinking hard. What a night! Where was the bastard camera phone when you need it?

Tamsin went to the toilet, a cold dark recess with red painted concrete floor and original sink and toilet complete with chain flush. John had conceded to put out some budget hand wash and a well-worn towel. Returning, she passed a fit couple of about 50, tanned as they were just back from their latest cruise.

"Drinks shorts is my advice", said Tracey Henderson, "saves you having to go so often."

Meanwhile Gervais had found the smoking den outside. Recently built of fresh untreated wood, it both smelt and looked like a Swedish sauna. To appease the smokers in the winter and stop them buying their beer at the supermarket and sitting in front of their own log fire, John had built in an electric heater on a pull string. Gervais was tempted to sprawl in just his pants and pour steaming water over the coals, but pulled himself together in time. Sitting puffing on a borrowed joint, Gervais began to enjoy his move to the country and began to swap stories about the area.

"Don't you be thinking of doing anything with that Romany Bubble land except putting sheep on it, there's black magic they say, only bad things come to those who try to develop it. I would put some beet in Long Bottom though, feed the sheep on it over winter and then plough and use for a summer crop and put the sheep in the valley." Gervais listened hard whilst he took another toke. He hoped he would remember all this advice in the morning.

"So, what do you miss about the city then G?" grinned one of the footballers. "Or rather – what am I missing by not being in the city?"

"Personal safety." Replied Gervais with a grin. "In London, I knew that the pavement was for people and the cars were for the road. Here, I have been run off the road by an attractive young lady in a tractor…"

"Sorry!" interrupted Sophie with a blond bobbed cheeky wave.

"I have been nearly knocked over by that bonkers horse that Phelps clings onto and don't get me started on those middle aged men in bright coloured lycra that go bombing past at all hours of the day. You can't bloody hear them and then whoosh you nearly lose a leg!" Everybody laughed.

"That bloody South Somerset cycle route can be a bit of a bind at times, but it brings in lots of pub trade," one of the older drinkers replied. "Anything else?"

"Oh, having nowhere but the pub to get cash, damn dangerous that, you get home and realise you still have an empty pocket despite drawing out £50! Hearing guns going off at all hours of the day and night, worse than Kingsland Road on a weekend! Worst of all though, is the lack of fast food delivery. You just have a few beers and want some kebab or something. You can't just pick up the phone, no you have to beg the wife to get in the car and drive to Martock! Otherwise, I have to say, it is bloody brilliant. I feel like I am on holiday all the time, walking down these pretty lanes, only half an hour or so to the Jurassic coast, the sound level is so much better and just the space is amazing!"

Meanwhile, Sarah slid up to Tamsin and slurred, "I've never met a girl like you before, and I thought you were a proper snob with your straight blond hair and designer jeans, but you are a great laugh. Fancy joining me on a Zumba course in London next week, reckon we could have a serious time!"

Before Tamsin realised what she was saying, she had let slip about the impending magazine visit.

"Yer, we prarper need to sort out yur 'ouse then." An older chap with a cider stretched belly popped over. "I' de send over miy Willy on Tuoosday, get thic waader a yours workin' again". Gervais raised half an ear at the word Willy. "Slip him a bit and I'll get some birds in on the game." Gervais began to get uneasy at the way the conversation was going and turned to join in. "There be fish in there waader if thic 'eron b'aint got em. I got lots of ducks needin an 'ome. We can git thic lake up an runnin' in no time. Wadder ya think?"

Before Tamsin could answer, she felt a harsh wide slap on her rump.

"Coor feeling fit you are, nice arse! Evening Gervais nice wife you got there!" One of the football team made his presence well known.

"We're off clubbin' mate, minibus is outside, two places spare if you fancy it? Sorted for E's and whiz, where the girls meet the boys and the boys meet the girls. Taun'on tonight".

Tamsin laughed.

"Not tonight, we have serious gardening to do to have the place ready by Wednesday when the press arrive."

"To the end!" came a shout; the pub haemorrhaged young men, pouring into a sliding door taxi. With a toot of the horn, the pub relaxed.

Clattering down the stairs, Clara had heard the noise of the evening and had pulled herself together to come down and see the night's entertainment. Heavily made up and wearing clothes a decade too old and a size too tight, she had covered her age with make- up. She had a sleazy past glamour about her that made her look full of exciting stories that you would love to hear.

"Evening all" she slurred. "Oh, you must be the pop stars over at Old Tom's? How are you finding it? Have you started renovating yet? Used to be a beautiful place in its time. A mini Montacute." She smiled politely and held out a tremulous hand.

"Clara, pleased to meet you." "I've been here a few years now, came from London myself. Always been in the business, takes a toll on your health I can vouch!"

Tamsin introduced herself and explained about the impending visit. Clara looked delighted and unconsciously began to pat her hair as if ready to meet the cameras. "Better get this place a bit more ship shape then, we don't want anyone reporting us to health and safety!" She cackled with an infectious laugh and Tamsin warmed to her, despite the state of the pub she kept.

Talk was rapid as everyone got excited and engaged about what the house and ground should look like and what everyone could do before the impending visit. Captain Phelps would ride past to set the scene and pop in with an early brace of pheasant. Season doesn't start for another three months but who cares! Willy would mow the lawns, tend the lake and bring over the ducks. Sarah would ensure lots of posters were up for the local drinking event in the village, Mark the local cider maker would drop of a few gallons of local scrumpy to have on offer. The plan was set.

Tamsin knew something was wrong.

She began to sway and black stars started to spot in front of her eyes. Christ, was this place more infected then she realised? Had the wine poisoned her?

She leaned to the side and vomited violently on the floor. Everyone roared with laughter. "Don't worry, Pam will sort that out."

Tamsin was confused, wasn't Pam the dog and Clara the land lady?

Pam bounced over looking livelier than she had in a few years and began to lick up the vomit. "Told you Pam would sort it! On this carpet, it is hidden anyway!"

Tamsin groaned. She was going to have to do something about the state of both herself and this pub before she could set foot in here again.

The night carried on into the small hours, lock- ins were a thing of the past. The doors were still shut and the curtains closed, but the police were not funded with the petrol to travel into villages in the dead of night and worry about late drinking now licensing laws were relaxed. Violence tended to be a town thing and the landlords and locals were quick to sort out any local disputes.

Staggering home in the moonless pitch dark night, Gervais and Tamsin crashed into each other and up the edges of the holloway where the road sank low and the trees made a huge arch, like a cathedral above. By day, it was a beautiful leafy tunnel. By night, it was black as pitch. Tripping into the ruts of the lane, they clutched at each other, roaring with laughter as they both fell onto the grass centred lane.

As they got closer to the house, they heard a deep scratchy man's cough. "What's that?" Gervais whispered, his heart racing. Tamsin was past hearing or caring and was getting out her giant iron key to open the huge oak door.

There was another cough and a shuffle of feet.

"Sounds like an old man. Hello? Who's there? Who is it? What do you want?"

Gervais was a little unnerved. In the old days, he had security around him, he was aware that his skills in self- defence were highly unlikely to be adequate here in the country.

Out of the darkness and shadows, Gervais just made out the outline of his black Welsh sheep. One of them opened his mouth and coughed again. Gervais chortled at his own inexperience and fear and crashed into the house.

"Come on sexy wife, most beautiful woman in the village, let me feel those pert breasts of yours." They tripped up the stairs, Gervais slapping Tamsin's behind as she raced in front of him. Tamsin popped into the bathroom to clean her teeth and when she came out, Gervais was snoring on top of the bed.

Chapter 7

Good as his word, when Tamsin peered out of the window on day two of her hangover, she was greeted by the sight of a strong muscular back as Willy began to mow the lawn.

Yawning, and still a little wobbly, she put on her satin robe and went downstairs to put on the coffee and get the post. She grimaced a bit when she saw the stack of bills for the local independent furniture shops and hoped to pay those before Gervais saw them.

She had been considering what to do about her little part of Romany's Bubble in the kitchen, the small babbling spring. It was beautiful now in the summer, but would the aga be good enough to keep the house warm when there was a constant flow of icy water? She didn't want to stop the ancient spring but was there a way of diverting it or boxing it in to make a cheap fridge?

Must chat to the locals, they seemed to know everything about this house. The idea of the curse on the land had made her shudder a little and she was determined to find out more with a little research sometime, after the magazine article.

A wave from Willy interrupted her thoughts. Instinctively she pulled her robe tighter and then waved back. She must get out in the garden and do some work today, but in the mean time she was happy to have a "Diet Coke moment" with her fresh coffee and muscular Willy.

It was yet another fine sunny day in Norton Beauchamp, something to do with how it lay in the lea of the hills kept it dryer and warmer than some of the other villages. Tamsin had learned to sleep with her window open so that she would wake up to the morning buzz of the country. In London, she would wake up to sirens, heavy traffic and constant building works. Here it was a riot of bird song, sheep baah, buzzard cries and the burbling of the chickens.

Filled with a true sense of wellbeing and feeling energised after the hell of yesterday's excruciating hang over, Tamsin began to plan what she wanted to say in her interview.

Gervais, who still had a bit of a head, was beginning to realise that he was not as young and fit as he used to be. Not that her was ever fit, he had kept his weight down with stimulants and not eating in the '90's. Looking at all the muscular builds around him had made him consider his life style. In the villages, everyone was reasonably fit, even the oldies were trim and up and out buy 8am, walking the dog or visiting their livestock. They had fresh glowing skin and a bounce about them. Most of the younger men were land workers, or ran and cycled. They seemed to be bucking the trend of obesity, where now in the early twenty first century, children were overweight by 10 and many people had faces grey and pock marked from a lack of healthy food and carried aprons of spare flesh. "I guess there is more to live for here." He mused.

"Today's gonna be the day!" Gervais got dressed and cursed when he saw Willy doing the lawn. He was hoping to slip off for a walk over the little brook that ran through the valley and see how safe the land was for building. He was debating whether to let it slip at the magazine interview and try to get the locals in a rage. Great publicity! Trouble was, he liked everyone here, they seemed honest helpful people. Is aggravating them his best plan of action?

Joining Tamsin for coffee, he padded down the stairs in CK PJ bottoms and wrapped himself around her. "Morning Honey" he snuffled into her neck. Tamsin curved her body into his and wrapped her arms backwards around his head, pushing forwards her breasts. "How do you fancy trying for a baby?" He ran his hands over her breasts through the silky fabric, feeling the nipples harden under his touch. "I see that Willy's doing the hard work outside, can mine do some hard work inside baby?" Putting down her coffee, she turned to face Gervais and slid off her robe. Excited at the thought of being watched by their gardener, he lifted her onto the table and slid up her nighty so that he could gently slide into her, full view to the window. Tamsin, still partially in her "Diet Coke" moment purred and wrapped her legs around him.

In the background Tamsin could hear the spring in the scullery bubbling ferociously and she began to feel her mouth dry and yearn for the bubbling on her tongue.

Helen meanwhile was looking out of the window and over the lea of the valley. She could see the outline of Willy with the lawnmower and smiled to herself. He got in there quickly, she thought with a smile. Pootle was fussing around her legs ever hopeful to be taken out for another walk. Helen felt the same and was trying to motivate herself to get out. The village shop might be a good place to start, get a paper and show her face. She wished she know what to say when people would ask why she wasn't at work, the truth would be sensible, always better to be honest. She knew that if she tried a "Captain Phelps" she would be laughed at. People can forgive struggle and failure; it makes them feel better about their own situations. They can't stand pretence.

It was another beautiful morning and Helen could not bear to be locked up any longer. A solitary fly buzzed around the cool kitchen reminding Helen that summer was here. Taking a deep breath and a dog lead and Waitrose carrier as a poo bag (she kept the Waitrose carriers but tended to bin the less salubrious ones), she was out of the door of Primrose Cottage. Strolling up the road, she took her time to allow the warmth of the early sun to filter into her bones. Cottages are cool in the summer, too cool sometimes, especially bare feet on flagstone floors…

The gardens sparkled fresh and new in the early sunlight, little balls of moisture cupped inside the petals of flowers glinted like diamonds and newly spun webs were sprinkled with jewels. Within the hour, all the dew would be gone and another hot day would preside. Many of the old houses were shrouded in wisteria with branches curved and wrapped, wriggling like snakes up the ham stone porches.

Helen was invigorated by the beauty of the day and swung happily into the shop almost forgetting herself. "Good Morning Helen, it's been a while since I have seen you. Are you ok?" Jane Phelps was always warm and welcoming. Helen felt herself melt. After the strict regime of school, someone who sounded like they genuinely cared, knocked Helen off guard. Tears sprung to her eyes and she swayed slightly. "Sweet heart, take a seat, whatever is the matter!" Gasped a concerned Jane. Helen burst into tears and the floodgates opened.

"Things will work out." Said Jane, soothingly. "Just take your time. You have 6 months on full pay before any crisis starts, so use them to get better. I'm always here if you need a chat. In fact, why don't you join the village committee? Get you out of the house and give you a focus. Good for the CV too a bit of volunteering. We have the village summer do to organise, we could do with your input on all the children's stuff. Here, why don't you come round the back for a bit, yes Pootle is fine too. Come and have a cuppa and put the worlds to right."

Helen emerged an hour later feeling a calm, almost serene state wash over her. She was able then to stride through the rest of the village with confidence and (almost) a smile on her face.

That evening, a lightness pervaded her soul that she hadn't felt in years. She was excited about getting herself ready to join the committee meeting in the pub. She was taking a little joy in deciding which scruffy jeans to wear. Knowing it didn't really matter but enjoying the ritual of getting ready to go out for the first time in ages.

She strolled up the old sheep drove towards the pub, enjoying the way the last embers of hot sun caused her brow to wrinkle, listening to the busy chatter of house martins as they begged their young to take that first leap into the air. It had been a generally good summer so far and nature seemed to be pleased with itself. She wandered through the wheat fields listening to the cracking of the ears warmed by the late sun, ready to be brought in by the huge mechanical beasts that blocked the roads in August. Pootle had chosen to come with her and was racing ahead with her pink tongue lolling out of her mouth.

Helen smiled, there must be life after teaching, but what could she do to envelop herself in this beautiful landscape that would pay the mortgage? She knew teaching was not an option. Even the thought of stepping in through the front gates filled her with a rising panic. She smiled ironically, knowing that as a child, she was never one of those for whom school was a daily fear, yet now as an adult, she was.

She pushed open the heavy oak of the pub door, swallowing her nerves and putting on a smile as she entered the sticky warm darkness.

"Hey it be our lovely 'elen. I ain't seen you 'ere for a bit, come on it. You 'ere for the committee meeting? They be out back. What can I get you my lovely?" John had heard about Helen's plight and being the carer of the family, he stretched an arm out to all his village flock (especially now the Vicar had four parishes to run and was stretched.)

Helen forced back the tightness of throat and the stinging rush to her eyes that she experienced when anyone was nice to her. "Pint of cider please John, and thank you."

"Right you are. Watch out now, I think my Clara migh' be coming down tonight, so remember don't take narfin' 'er says to 'eart, her forgot 'ow to be pleasant when 'er took up drinkin the profits."

Helen giggled and thanked John, noting inside that life seems to be a struggle for so many people. Just when you think someone has got the world and you allow yourself a little jealousy at the comfort of their lives, you realise that they are struggling too in some way.

Helen dipped her head to pass into the old lady's lounge. It was no better decorated than the rest of the pub, tatty patterned old pub carpet and dark wooden furniture that Helen remembered from her childhood. Horse brasses and football cups piled on the alcoves of the inglenook fireplace, black with soot from the fire. Inside she could see a group of heads muttering over their pints and she glanced over to see whom she recognised. Having grown up in the village, she knew nearly everyone but had not met them socially since her parents passed away. She suddenly felt a bolt of fear. What would people say to her?

Jane raised her head first. "Hey Helen, really pleased you could make it. Come and join us. I've got you a chair here. Good. Glad you got a drink in."

Helen glanced round. The Hendersons were there, tanned and round after another cruise. Phelps in countryside green, Tom and Estella Wesley the young couple who owned the posh Georgian house with huge manicured grounds. Lottery winners, was the general thoughts about their income as they always seemed to be about in the village and not tied to long hours away working like most people in decent houses. There was the fitness lady, Sarah, looking lovely as usual.

"Do you know everyone?" Jane made the introductions and everyone made the appropriate nods and murmurs. "Well as you know we are getting on with our late summer show plans. We have the Vicar organising the parachute jump from the top of the tower, Tracey are you still ok with the children's street party? I am sure you can have a chat with Helen in a minute, she will have some great ideas about entertainment and crowd control. How is the customised wheel barrow race coming on, I hear that we are having police and insurance issues about making it start and finish at the pub? How about the on street Bokwa Sarah? Should be a laugh with a few of those scrumpies we have got from the cider mill."

The organisation was taking place quickly and everyone was being assigned jobs.

"We are going to book some bands. The local brass band will play in the afternoon and we thought we would book the Mangelwurzels, you know, the Wurzels cover band. Do you think we need a simple covers band too?"

Shane piped up "What 'bout them new pop stars down Old Tom's? Would be quite a pull to git 'im on stage, we could let slip to the press an sell us stories? Make a few pennies on the side for 'ee."

"Great idea Shane, who knows them well enough to persuade them? Brilliant Tom and Estella, invite them over to dinner and drop it into the conversation!"

They all stopped to gather new pints and the conversation was raised again. "John, are you going to put on some food for the evening, or do we need to engage the deli in something?"

At that moment, Clara came clattering down the stairs. Her hair was pulled in a bun on her head rather hastily and her heavy black eye makeup had begun to travel south.

"Evening you lot. John, I hope you aren't agreeing to doing any food. This is a pub; we don't cater for family events. You all expect too much. I hope you have got some chemi- lavs booked because I am not having all and sundry traipsing through the bar using our services. We spend a bomb on toilet paper as it is."

"Shame 'ee don't spend more on toilet cleaner as well as paper" remarked Shane as he began to roll up a cigarette with yellow stained fingers.

"Don't worry I'm going outside with it!"

Everyone turned and stared in surprise at Clara and John raised his eyes in apology.

"The pub is for drinking only and mark my words don't think I haven't noticed how you use it as a meeting room and sit there with one pint between you all."

Everyone looked at their second pints and back at Clara who turned with a wobbly flourish, pushing John cruelly out of the way and marched out of the room. The door slammed and the stamps up the stairs were only interrupted by a slip and a clatter. Even Pam raised her dull eyes up from her nightly drip tray at the sound.

"I'm sorry, 'er is getting worse. I don't know what to do with 'er, this place is falling down around us but she won't budge. She ain't understood bout a pub bein' for the 'ole village, 'er still lives in the years of men only pits. I would like to shove 'er in a man only pit I can tell 'ee."

Everyone laughed politely but none had an inkling of the beating John was in for tonight, or for what the future held.

The meeting wound up and Helen walked home with Tracey Henderson, discussing children's entertainment and tricks to keep arguments low and safety high.

Chapter 8

It was the day of the press interview and Tamsin had spent much of the previous night painting her walls and afterwards her nails. She had completed a final walk about the house and the grounds and was pleased that things were ok. Willy's ducks had taken to the newly cleared out lake and she loved listening to them wake her up in the morning. They set a rural sense of calm, as did the sheep in the field.

"Please God let me get this right and not be the laughing stock of the press."

In the scullery, the spring answered by bubbling gently against the stones.

Gervais was doing much the same, walking nervously around his livestock, again placing hen's eggs to boost his stock and laying a trug he had bought from Waitrose next to the runner beans that Willy had set up for him. "God make this work; help me get the recognition we need. Help me pay those bloody furniture companies, and God remind me to take a closer notice of where Tamsin buys things."

A brand new shiny BMW X5 pulled into the drive and out hopped two glamorous women and a young shorthaired man with a huge bag of camera equipment. They hovered outside chatting for a few moments before walking tentatively in heels up the freshly weeded gravel drive and knocked on the huge oak door.

"Darling, just look at you! The countryside seems to have you positively blooming! Mwah Mwah Oh sorry darling it is three now, Mwah I have been summering on the continent. Gosh what a gem, how old is this? It looks like that big National Trust house down the road where they filmed Wolf Hall."

Tamsin let everyone in and found herself caught up in a whirlwind of dressing, make – up and a flurry of questions. "God please make me have answered these ok."

"Darling please, in front of that beautiful aga, and where is that delicious husband of yours. Gervais, you must come and hold her by that lovely oak dresser. Is it an original by any chance? Ooh bespoke, lovely. Any patter of tiny feet yet? What are you thinking – private or village school?

Oh, Gervais I suppose we had better venture out onto that God forsaken farm of yours.

Callum, can you go out with him and take a picture with some sheep or something?"

Gervais and Callum strode out whilst Gervais spoke about the trials of gathering live- stock and the mixed blessing of the continuous call of the rooster. They walked over to the lake that linked onto Romany Bubble.

Callum remarked on the stunning, gently folding hills and the plantation that run alongside. Gervais began again to consider his desire to build, and passed a remark to Callum. "Can you imagine five top class houses on there, lawns gently sloping to the river? Beautiful. All local stone of course and perhaps a shared swimming pool in the grounds. Callum muttered and the moment passed.

That evening Tamsin and Gervais shared a bottle of Prosecco.

"Hopefully this will soon be Cristal again." They had made enough money to rebuild the cow shed with the aim of bringing on bullocks over the winter to sell for meat in the spring. There would be some left over for Gervais to approach the solicitors about the covenant and how expensive it could be to remove. They had sent the reporter off with "Free range "eggs that Gervais had cunningly placed in their coop earlier and the ideas of planting home field as an orchard to rival the local niche cider producer who sold to China, courtesy of his London links and spent the summer selling at festivals including Glastonbury only 10 miles up the road.

"God, you looked sexy in that red underwear they put you in. Go and put some more on and tell me all about what they said to you when they took your photo."

Buoyed up on excitement and a bottle of Prosecco, Tamsin obliged and sat on his lap drinking Prosecco from the bottle until it spurted from her lips. Gervais ran his tongue over hers and begged her to tell him more about Callum's words. Tamsin spread her legs wider and leant her pushed up breasts closer to Gervais. "Oh beautiful" she slurred, "That's so sexy, now show me more honey, that's it, work that body." Gervais obliged.

A rumpled Tamsin with breasts still half pushed out of her red balconette bra wondered downstairs to see the note on the mat. "Hmm dinner at the Wesley's tonight, that could be nice. She was still slightly drunk from the night before and returned to bed to see if the bra could work the magic effect of the night before.

Gervais was up and in the shower. "I'm off to the solicitors today. Gonna find out about that covenant. Can't be hard to lift and I want to make some money!" He gulped down the stinging hot coffee, slowly and languorously kissed Tamsin, run his hands under her G-string, and then bounced out of the door, roaring away in the SUV.

Tamsin finished a leisurely breakfast, changed the red for a more comfortable set of underwear and went for a stroll around the farm, tickling the sheep and collecting the hen's eggs. She paused to look at Romany's Bubble valley and calculated whether the houses would be a total eyesore. The view for her would be fine, but for those cottages over there, she was not so sure. One belonged to the Hendersons; they would be fine because they were always on holiday, but what about the other one? She had seen a girl and a poodle come in and out on a few occasions but knew little more.

She turned her mind to the invitation from the Wesley's. She quite looked forward to seeing their Georgian Mansion. "Well, if they can get that rich from property development, why can't we?" She mused. She went upstairs to turn out a long summer dress that would drape over her slim lines and reveal some leg. "I rather like that Tom Wesley. Wonder if they have a hot tub…"

Estella had decided to buy in. The deli in the next village had a line of cooks who would prepare to order and she decided on monkfish with lemon and new potatoes. The deli was renowned for its superb deserts so she had left the rest to Deli Amanda to decide upon. The cleaner was due, so all she had to do was set the table and decide on the wine and the music. It would be good to get to know Gervais and Tamsin better, she reasoned. They seemed up for a laugh. Perhaps they would bring something extra with them to get the party started, or perhaps they could get them in the hot tub for some fun. She wandered through her extensive walk in wardrobe and landed on a low cut classy summer evening dress. She had more boobs than Tamsin and she was going to make the most of them!

Boyed up on the success of the previous evening, Gervais was slightly bullish at the solicitors. They pored over the contracts and the deeds and could find nothing about a covenant. It seemed that there had been settlements on the land dating back 200 years that had been torn down and not rebuilt, but no actual written covenant. The farm had been passed to Tom 60 years ago. He had kept the place as a wild life sanctuary, grazing sheep only. But no statement to say he couldn't build…

Gervais was determined to ask the villagers more about the land and scope out their response to planning permission before he began any expensive proceedings. "Bugger!" he shouted out loudly as he realised he was out at the Wesley's that night. He was hoping to slip down to the pub and begin asking around whilst people had some of the strong stuff flowing in their veins.

Dinner started sedately. Gervais and Tamsin were welcomed with a kiss to each cheek and a glass of champagne. Gervais and Tamsin felt a bit guilty about their offerings of supermarket sauvignon blanc and chocolates.

"So lovely to have you join us. I am afraid I have cheated a little; you will be relieved to hear that Deli Amanda has created the menu, not me! I have a beautiful kitchen but I am not great at utilizing it!

Have you tried her food before? She really is superb, runs the deli in the next village."

Tamsin looked up at the large hall painted in that beautiful grey blue with white coving and old hunting pictures.

"Got those at the antique shop in Crewkerne. Us nouveaux – riche, have to start somewhere! What's the point of being rich, if you don't know what to do with it?" Would you like to have a look around?

Tamsin followed Estella into the beautiful oak bespoke painted country kitchen. It is the style that most people lust after and then purchase the cheap version at the chain kitchen fitter companies. Full of locally woven baskets and beautiful cookware and of course a huge aga.

"That is just for show," admitted Estella. "It takes too long for me. We use it to heat the place in the winter, but I have a good bottled gas hob and electric oven."

The idea of bottled gas intrigued Tamsin. She had not been amused by the lack of mains gas in the village. Heating was with oil and cooking was with electricity. They had been weighing up the idea of solar panels on the house, or perhaps their own solar farm as many of the local farmers had. But this was a revelation. Until she realised the price…

The bathrooms were decorated in the Georgian style with chequered floors and marble fittings. The house was much grander and less characterful than Manor Farm and although Tamsin admired it, she thought their antique painted half- timbered walls were probably the correct design for them. She did however like the way the evening sun filtered through the huge windows. The tiny ham stone mullioned windows of Manor Farm let in little light and warmth.

They sat in the cream sofas of the drawing room with their champagne and began to swap stories of the past and the gossip of the village. Tamsin decided quickly to watch what she drank, as she didn't want to reveal her less than salubrious past.

"Have you heard the latest exploits of those gyppo's down on the moors? Apparently, they have been pinching the chickens and making it look like the fox has dug through. Then they have tried to sell reinforced fencing whilst reselling the chickens to other people who they have pinched off. Great scam but they have cameras at Orchard Farm…

Dave and Jill went after them with their rifles and sorted it. Mind you, I hear there was some bare knuckle fighting to settle the argument. God, it is like the old days! No wonder no-one wants them living near you. You would have to nail everything down!"

Tamsin giggled and thought they sounded as resourceful as the East Enders who got her modelling. Where there is a need, there is a way.

Gervais wondered how much cameras would cost. He knew that sheep rustling was a problem.

The wine flowed and the conversation became more raucous. Tamsin forked up the sundried tomato and parmesan ribbons from her salad and decided country life was definitely as refined as city life. She was loving it.

Tom smuggled the performance question in carefully. He was getting Gervais excited by the good old days. "Did you ever do solo's you know without the band, a capella or un plugged, you know?" Gervais pictures the days of jumping up and down on the spot, shouting into the microphone and wondered if he had the skill to sing alone. Before he knew it, he had agreed to sing at the local village fete and play his acoustic guitar.

Bang!

Gervais was awake. He peered through sticky eyes, trying to locate his surroundings before the shards of light pierced into his brain. He could just make out the soft breathing that he knew belonged to Tamsin. Opening his eyes a little further he could isolate the oak panels of his room.

He had made it home.

Breathing a sigh of relief, he closed his eyes again. His stomach buckled forcing him to sit up.

What had he agreed to last night? Oh God he said he would sing in front of the village!

Not having the energy to do anything else, Gervais reclosed eyes, to emerge late into the afternoon.

The same Sunday morning, Jane opened the papers to enjoy a cursory read before she sold them to the villagers. Her eyes swept over the small print, looking for something of interest.

His eyes became focused on the shape of a familiar name and she began to read.

What a Gervais Cock- up!

Gervais "Cock" James formally of the 90's Britt Pop band "Squelch" and his beautiful ex-model wife Tamsin moved to his new very big house in the country in May, to start a rural idyll based on farming. Tamsin has carefully renovated the Tudor Manor Farm in South Somerset with a sensitive and stylish interior, (See July issue of Country Sights for photos and article,). Gervais has decided to side step the slow development of his livestock and is going for a quick buck by building executive homes for posh people on a most beautiful steep sided valley. (Known as "Combes" in the South West). I wonder what the locals are going to make of that!

The local area has a shortage of affordable homes so the children of the villagers have to move to the local towns to live. The properties that Gervais outlined to me when I interviewed him in his Somerset mansion recently are most certainly not to support the local community. These will be for the more advantaged few. Perhaps Londoners seeking a new rural life like himself.

Use social media to let us know what you think of Gervais's ideas, is he right or is it a total outrage?

Captain Phelps whistled, "Oh dear, the fat is in the fire me thinks. Whatever is he thinking? Still that won't get past planning."

"Not if I have anything to do with it." Said Jane firmly. "Right I feel another committee coming on."

Captain Phelps shifted uncomfortably. "Gosh I hope I didn't have anything to do with it, I told him he might be able to lift the covenant on the land. I meant for grazing livestock, not building bloody great posh houses!"

Jake was sitting in his caravan on a layby. The road was full of speeding cars rushing down to Lyme Regis for a warm evening on the cobb and the noise was deafening. He had finally been evicted again and had nowhere to go. He had nowhere but the verges to graze the ponies and he hated the thought of the exhaust the children were breathing in.

"At least there isn't any lead in it anymore" he consoled himself. 'Enry wrapped himself around his legs grunting as he had nowhere comfortable to flop. In the summer, he loved the grassy cool under the caravan. But this place lent itself only to pools of oil and the stench of old urine.

"Yer!Look at this" Eli waved the local newspaper at Jake. "Seems there be trouble down at Old Romany's Bubble. Thic Popstar with the funny name wants to build 'ouses on it. Don't 'ee know that's against the old rules? 'Aint no-one put 'ee straight? Reckon we might 'ave to do some protesting. Burst 'ees bubble wone it! You up for a peaceful sit in? Gotta be bedder than sitting on this dirty great road any'ow!

It was one of those hot stifling nights. Helen lay in bed with just a sheet over her. She had the window open and was listening to the scolding blackbirds and the repetitive bars of the nightingale's four beat ditties. The sun had left pale pink and yellow folds on the horizon like the ice cream coloured row of beach huts at Lyme Regis.

She turned over and closed her eyes. Sleeping was coming easier these days and didn't take a bottle of wine to achieve. She had taken to running early in the morning, when no one was yet around and she found it was agreeing with her.

She fell into a gentle dream where she was walking over the hills, overlooking the cliffs when Poldark appeared over the horizon on his beautiful black cob. There was a bumping grinding noise and the rattle of broken metal dragged over hard earth. Both she and Poldark turned to look. There was a whinny of a pony and the thump of feet on the ramp of a transporter. Then the dream melted away and Helen reached peaceful sleep.

She was woken as usual at 5am by the sun streaming in her window. It was easy to get up at 5am when you did not have to go to work. You knew you could go back to sleep at any time during the day and there was no sense of deep exhaustion as you try to pull yourself from much needed rest into the speed and stress of the workload ahead. Helen pulled on her trainers and running gear.

"Right Mum, time to get up and get out, I know you would do the same." No need to get washed as no one would see. Today would be over Romany's Bubble and through the forest beyond.

She loved pacing through the sweet-smelling pine tracks, following "The Bubble" against its busy flow down to the valley. It broke into tiny waterfalls and made a constant babble as it gathered pace over the deep narrow carving it had created.

"Guess that is where the name came from". Helen pondered aloud. The gypsies certainly had frequented the area in the past before they were evicted. In the old days, they would gather at harvest time and camp there ready to undertake the seasonal bean picking in Martock. Once it was over they would travel further through North Somerset or over to Wiltshire ready for the harder work of beet and winter cabbages.

As she circled at the top of the hill and broke into the sunshine of the valley, she thought she saw something glint in the morning light. Running fast, enjoying the way gravity allowed her to pick up long fast paces, she crashed to the bottom of the valley and thundered to the marshy bottom. Suddenly she realised she wasn't alone.

Pulling on the brakes and sliding down the steep slope, Helen fell to her knees in a messy pile. Looking up to see what had disturbed her, she saw three huge shiny white caravans and a collection of white vans and a 4wd. Peering back up at her was an old skewbald pony and an even older grey lurcher. Backing up hastily she reversed, maintaining her eye on the growling dog and the grass-cropping skewbald. A curtain twitched. Helen leaped up and ran.

"That must have been the noises in my dream last night," she realised. Rather embarrassed about her behaviour (and the hotter parts of her dream), she blamed it on the caravan dwelling intruders for taking over her favourite run.

"Ok good to have you all here again, thank you for coming" Jane broke the general hubbub of the fete organisers. "Well are we all set for this weekend? I can't believe we are here already, August again, the fields are almost all cut thanks to the good weather we have been having and it is set to be dry for the party at the weekend!"

"Tom and Estella! Congratulations on achieving us rather a memorable band for the day. And as talented as they are, I don't mean the Kingsbury Episcopi band booking either!" Everybody erupted into cheers.

"Arthur, have we ever had a pop star in the village before?"

It was the day that Arthur and some of the other older residents were brought to the pub by the volunteer transport scheme. They would play cards and finish a bottle of Port between them. Arthur, an ex-spitfire pilot was able to hold his drink and stay awake far longer than the others. They had been transported back hours earlier! Arthur was contenting himself with a chat to whoever came in and with the occasional doze. He still had that wonderful upper class voice. Phelps would listen carefully to the old chap who was everything he wanted to be.

"Ha ha, don't forget thic Wurzel cover band. Tis Mangle Wurzels innit! They have been playing in here and in the local meadows many a time! Can't beat a jolly night with a pint and a song!"

Shane was the opposite of Arthur.

"So, the line- up is like this", interrupted Jane.

"Children's street tea and the old people's tea dance to the Kingsbury Episcopi band at 12.30. We all will help set up and clear down.

Church parachuting bears at one – I hear there is going to be a death slide for some as well! Who is going up the church tower to drop them off? You game old Jim?"

Jim burbled with laughter and ended up in a bout of coughing until his face was glowing and ruddy and tears rolled down his cheeks.

"Cor tis years since I been able to do nothing like that, but I'll tell ee, my Willy be up there quicker than no other!"

Everyone roared at the unintended double- intender and agreed they would put his Willy up the church tower to throw his teddies.

"Ok" sobbed Jane holding her sides, "The café is opening for cream teas and ice cream, is that right? Oh, and some tapas as well, lovely.

Pony rides are on from twelve to two – I will do that with our Shetland Grumph, while Phelps sorts out the magician. Perhaps he can cast a spell on our Betsey, Nutcase. Speaking of which, Helen, Phelps wanted a chat with you about Bets sometime, he could do with your expertise. Right sorry back to it.

We all put out the tables in the street from 3pm; we have sold every single one as usual.

Then Shane it is you with the wheelbarrow race up and down the road closure area at 4pm and the Mangle Wurzels play at six to get everyone up here with their byo and picnics.

Sarah will do her Zumba or Bokwa or whatever it is, at 8pm and then it is a short break before Gervais will play at 9.

Hopefully everyone will help us clear up and put the tables away, amazing how much strength and energy some people have after a few of the local brew.

Now onto something I want to show you all. It's for discussion after this weekend is over, we can't think too much about it now, but has anyone seen this?"

She unfolded and wiped straight the newspaper cutting about Gervais's building intentions and tilted it on the table for maximum viewing.

"Cheeky bastard!" exclaimed Shane as he read aloud the subheading.
"Whaaat a Gervais Carck- up!"

"Not Romany's Bubble!" gasped Helen. "No way! It's not possible! Is that what I saw down there the other day then? I thought it was gypsies passing through like they sometimes do, being their old harvest stop off."

"Not a word to anyone!" Urged Tom, "Let's keep it to ourselves for the moment. I am sure we can prevent this happening, but we will need the element of surprise on our side. Please say nothing, I will look into the planning regs and covenant and see what I can find out. Once the party is over we can get our heads together."

"I agree" said Phelps, "not a word to anyone yet, we may need to be cunning and devious to win this one." Call me a NIMBY if you want but there 'aint no posh development going up on my watch!"

"Tis 'ouses for the villagers 'us needs. Something we can afford in a place that won't offend no-one. Not gert poshuns for the likes of 'ee Londoners." Shane agreed.

"Time you sorted out that front drive of yours if you don't want to offend anyone! How many car bits and oily tarpaulins have you got up there now?" Tom grinned at Shane with more than a jovial hint.

Everyone cheered and banged their pints on the table causing Clara to raise her drunken head off the pillow upstairs and even Pam the flatulent black lab to raise her head from snuffling the drip trays.

Chapter 9

Tamsin popped into Yeovil and bought her edition of "Country Sights" when it came out. She hadn't made front cover, but she had a 4-page spread. She didn't care too much as the money was in the bank. Or rather in the creditors banks by now. She flipped through the photo's quickly and saw that they were all flattering. "Thank you!" she whispered.

She stopped in one of the new organic/ healthy/vintage style tearooms that seemed to be popping up everywhere and ordered a cup of Earl Grey. She didn't miss the wheat grass smoothie culture and couldn't find bitter green shakes in the least bit appealing. She knew she was lucky that dieting had never been a necessity for her and she dabbled with health food to maintain a fresh complexion only.

She settled and started to read.

"*Ninety's model Tamsin Martin is as beautiful as the roses that frame her Tudor farmhouse in Somerset. She has taken to the country life like her ducks to the water on her restored millpond. We wonder if there will be the patter of tiny feet on those cool flagstone floors.*

In the footsteps of some eminent TV stars and reputedly a US film star, South Somerset and West Dorset are the place to be. Setting up a small farm with her pop star husband Gervais Martin, famous for his tongue in cheek melodies of 90's culture, Tamsin seems the perfect country wife and her home is a beauty.

When asked about the designers she has used, Tamsin said, "I have not chosen to go with an expensive designer, but have scoured the area for local tradesmen and crafts people. I feel it gives the house an authentic feel and returns it to where it came from, with a few modern comfort twists of course." She laughs. "The area is full of artists and crafts people. It is such a pleasure to live here. I have been so lucky to be able to take a wreck and use locals to create that past feel. "

We certainly agree as Tamsin walked us through her idyllic farmhouse…

The passage was rather gushing and so Tamsin thought it would be good to pop a copy in the shop window, or in the pub for others to read. They didn't say much about the village though, if was focussed on her and the house. Perhaps she could move to another lifestyle magazine now and see if she could put more of the villagers in.

Little did Tamsin know that the newspaper article that has quietly passed her by had aroused the suspicion and planning of the locals and that she may not be quite so well received in the future.

Helen had been up to see Phelps to help him lunge Betsy with a view to calming her enough to teach her some manners. She had been surprised at how the smell of horse had jolted he senses and memories, making her feel peaceful and complete. She enjoyed chatting to Phelps as she whisked and scraped the body brush and curry comb in that simple rhythm that came back as naturally as breathing.

"Have you seen much of Gervais and Tamsin, Helen?" Phelps enquired. "You can see the farm from the back of yours, can't you?"

"Oh yes I have been watching things progress, the ducks are lovely to watch as they waddle up to the island in the pond. It has been a pleasure watching it all come back to life. From the outside, it all looks rather nice. I haven't met them yet though, what about you?"

Phelps thought hard. He hadn't been able to make a great judgement on Tamsin; she didn't give a lot away. She tended to look pretty and do the right things, but rarely would you see her compromised and she didn't reveal much about herself.

His male interest had, been awoken. As much as he loved Jane, he had married her because she loved him and could introduce him to the country life. Renovating the barn that had belonged to her family had been a help. She was safe, comforting and loveable, but she had never excited him. Being on close contact with Tamsin had awoken feelings inside he had put to one side.

Jane had comfortably responded to his recent advances but he had to keep himself in check.

"Gervais is ok. Bit full of it as you would expect, but he seems to really enjoy drinking with the boys. He wants to make a go of that farm, but I think he is all about making enough money to live in the quickest way he can rather than really being a farmer. I know they have had young Willy over there helping out a bit, that's how the lake and ducks go sorted so quickly.

Tamsin, she's pretty and agreeable. Haven't seen much of a personality, she tends to shy away from giving of herself. Bit boring really. People are much more fun when they let their hair down. I think I should make that my quest. See what she is really about, whether this farming lark is for her, or will she run back to city once the fine weather is over."

Helen laughed, "Reckon you need to focus on *this* mare first!" She had put Betsy onto the lunge rein and was encouraging her to walk and then trot and then walk again without moving to the jog that she was sticking to on the road. She worked her on each rein, changing her direction to exercise the muscles on both sides and to stop her getting dizzy. She made Betsy think about what she was being asked and soon the horse that could jog sideways for hours was beginning to perspire.

She took her over to the wall, used it as a mounting block to jump on, and adjusted her stirrups and girth. Next, she started working Betsy in the same manner around the field. Making her think carefully about what was being asked. Collected walk, extended walk, collected trot, change rein, back to the walk, onto a trot. Reining back, extended trot.

"Take her for a walk down the road. Don't let her trot. Once you are back giving her the orders you will be boss again."

15 minutes later both Phelps and Betsy returned perspiring and they both made use of the hose in the stable yard.

"Not bad!" Phelps grinned, "It took some work but we kept to it. Same again tomorrow? You are a star, thank you." He gave Helen a quick hug and she wandered home feeling warm with being useful again. "Till tomorrow." She whispered

Meanwhile John was taking stock of his miserable existence and considering what would be his best move. He couldn't stay in the abusive situation, yet he was aware of the man he had become. Weak, talentless, useless and worthy of no more than being a punch bag. Hell, he couldn't even stand up to a drunk woman and he wasn't even man enough to do anything about it.

He sighed deeply as he looked around his dull and dirty pub. He needed to do something soon, but Clara refused to spend money on the place and less and less people were using it. The locals only did because it meant they could drink in the village and then not have to drive home. Clara refused to go out and see what the competition looked like, but from what he had seen on his travel to Bookers to buy toilet roll and crisps, his pub was sadly lacking.

He considered whether to contact their son, who had disappeared to Australia and, apart from the occasional email, John's only information about his Alex was what John could decipher from his Facebook account.

No one to talk to, nowhere to go but something had to change. John began to fantasize about life without Clara. Her life insurance would pay the mortgage and sort out the decoration. How could he do it? He knew it was only fantasy, but what if?

Was there a way of making her drink stronger so she died of alcohol poisoning? No one would question that. Perhaps if he spiked her second bottle of wine with vodka, and maybe her third. By then she wouldn't be aware of it and then "Bob's your uncle."

John began to draw the new bitter through the cleaned lines with added ferocity, a wry sort of half grin on his face as he began his fantasy again.

Phelps was wrapped in his own fantasy as he walked Aga the black lab on their usual route round the fields, or for Aga up and down the maize rows leaping high between them as he caught a scent. Their walk always wound up for a pint at the pub and Phelps aware of their finances was astute at sticking to the one on weekdays.

His fantasy was based in a tall thin blond with no discernible face, but a figure reminiscent of Tamsin. Being a romantic at heart, it started with rose covered walks and pints of cider before descending into wandering hands slipping under braless t-shirts and wandering up free flowing loose gypsy style skirts. He was quite lost in thought as Aga dragged him through the oak door and into the gloom of the pub.

"Evening Phelps, your usual?"

"Evening John, yes please." The glorious reverie was broken and the tightness in his pants slowly loosened as Phelps returned to the day in hand.

"Any exciting news on the grapevine, John?"

"Not as yet, though I reckon you might 'ave sommat to tell I though?"

"Urm really? Why's that?"

"I saw 'ee with that young 'elen t'other day an' again today. What you up to, you sly old dog?"

They both laughed.

"No, the lovely Helen has been sorting out my not so lovely Betsy for me. We have got her a bit calmer through lunging and some manners teaching."

"Is that where yee put 'er on a big bit a rope and whip 'em till they do as they be told?"

Both men took a sip of their drinks and their minds drew a picture of whipped mares. Tamsin tied to a bed in a red room reminiscent of Mr Grey's and Clara whipped until she promised never to hit him again.

"So 'ow is our 'elen. She getting any bedder? 'er looked brighter when I saw 'er in the shop t'other day. Good to see her thrivin' I were a bit worried about 'er."

Yes, she is a bit brighter. Still very down on herself. Thinks she is a failure because she doesn't see herself returning to teaching. I think she should do more with the horses. I know the money is no good, but she is such a talent and she just loves being out in the countryside. Then we need to get her a nice man. None of those daft footballers, they are not ready for someone as gentle and sensitive as Helen."

"Oooh 'ave you got a crush on our young 'elen?"

"Don't be daft, she is like a daughter to us, Jane and I, we really felt for her when her parents died. She has really been through the mill. She could do with something or someone good happening in her life. I want to get her out more so that she has the opportunity to meet someone or hear about a different life chance for her. Staying in will get her nowhere. She has had a month now of staying in apart from those couple of summer party meetings. That's enough head burying time. Life will start again whether she likes it or not!"

Both men sighed and considered their own lives. John, realising that he was doing a Helen, except that he had been hiding his problems for years. Phelps wishing, he could stop hiding under the façade he had created for himself.

"Ye 'eard any more 'bout them gyppo's?" John asked at last.

"Absolutely, I hear they have left the road side they were being evicted from. Helen reckons they are pitched up on Romany's Bubble. Makes sense, it has been gypsy stop over land for years. I confess I haven't been over there for a while but maybe I should. Ha ha! Can't imagine what Gervais would make of that. Mind you, it will put a scupper on his development plans if he has to get rid of squatters. Hmm speaking of which, I wonder if they have any squatter's rights, seeing as it is traditional gypsy land."

"We could get 'em to perpetuate the myth of the curse. Get 'em to play a few tricks or do some chanting or sommat to scare off the developers."

Both men chuckled.

"Right that's me done. See you tomorrow." Phelps drained his glass and strolled off with Aga at his heels.

Gervais had been considering the village summer party with dread. Why the hell had he got so drunk? Why did he allow his own daft vanity to get him into this situation? Inter band arguments about the cuts of royalties had left him and the other three band members on bad terms with a court agreement splitting the royalties and stopping them from playing together again. That meant, gulp that Gervais would have to play alone with just his guitar.

Gervais knew he was not that great. He was not Ed Sheeran with a guitar by any long stretch of the imagination. He was going to have to get to work.

Dusting off the old musical scores and reminding himself of the old tracks, he began to work on creating a melody that would create a feeling of the old music without needing all the other instruments. He had written the lyrics in the old days but the music was not his skill. This was going to take a while. Thank God, this was just a small village event and not Glastonbury Festival just up the road.

Meanwhile, gentle Jane was getting a little crafty. Quietly enraged by the newspaper article and angry that Gervais would come down and impose his

London ways on a lifestyle that had functioned very well thank you for years without him, she was going to get some revenge.

Knowing that publicity for his project would fuel plenty of opposition and that having him play in the village would certainly gain publicity, she had contacted the local press and the newspaper that had carried his development story. Both were on their way to the summer party. No one else knew and she was not about to tell anyone.

It could go well but it could go so wrong. Not used to dealing with fire, Jane felt a little flutter or excitement and power within her.

Chapter 10

It was 2 days until the end of summer village party. Most of the fields had been harvested. The huge green monsters were illuminating the night, roaring up and down the fields like a cyclopoid leviathan.

Throughout the August days, cars were required to reverse miles down the narrow lanes as the cylindrical bales of straw were hauled by the huge tractors to be stored for bedding. Some were stacked 10-foot-high and driven at speed down the A303 whilst their heavily laden trailers would shed and whip straw into the windscreens of the cars behind. Others were left golden and round in the fields like ancient monuments to Sun Gods, standing in solemn rows as the heavy late summer sun glinted on the stubble left behind.

If you looked carefully into the cab of Sophie's huge blue tractor, you would see Willy flipping through Facebook on his phone as the new machinery used satellite navigation to cut the grains in a straight row. Willy's presence was only to oversee the process and to stop if the grain lorries behind became out of sync.

A buzz of expectation had grown over the village. Everyone loved the party. It was a great time for the children and adults alike to get together. The children loved playing out unattended until after dark, taking bets to see if they were brave enough to run through the churchyard and they enjoyed the chance to lie in the centre of the road, in the way some of the harder drinkers might end up later.

Tables were bought and prepared with delicious selections of Spanish and Italian meats from Lidl, specialist tomatoes and bread from the farmers markets. Deli Amanda and the café worked hard to produce the hot tapas and everyone contributed to the street party menu, from a packet of salt and vinegar to exquisite fairy cakes piled on Cath Kidston table wear.

The day dawned brightly. John took the chance to make sure there was plenty of toilet paper and cleaning fluids in the cubicles, in the hopes that people would take it upon themselves to clean up any mess they made. He lovingly prepared the curry to the instructions on the back of the packet and left it to simmer. Clara stayed in bed until her head began to subside and then she decided to make herself look beautiful.

John had asked a few villagers to help behind the bar. Sue who cleaned the village hall, shop and the pub to fund her single parent family would be a safe bet, so would the Henderson's 19-year-old daughter back from university. He idly wondered whether today would be the day to add the vodka? Perhaps there would there be too many people who might revive her. Laughing at his wicked thoughts, he checked all the gas was at the correct level so he would not lose too much to wastage.

Gervais took a huge breath. He had been practicing his gig ever since he drunkenly agreed to it. The planned performance was ok, but not great. Would it be it a good idea to get drunk and then blame it on that, or should he stay sober enough to remember some of the hard work he had put in.

Tamsin had far less stressful things on her mind as she decided on a summer dress that would take her through the day, look summery and causal but carefully tailored to make the most of her slight figure.

Helen had been busy helping with the street party food and the entertainers. She set up her face-painting stall and the chalk ready for the road art competition. She chose jeans and a bright dotty shirt. She had carefully painted a rose on her face to demonstrate her capabilities. A flutter of excitement went through her. It was the day where she would see everyone. There would be no hiding after this. Everyone would know her fate. God what would Claire, the other teacher in the village say, would she laugh at her, or think her weak and useless? Bet she had a promotion to go with my failure. Her stomach twisted with a ferocity that took her by surprise. She took a sip of her water and told herself off.

"How you react to something is up to you. Ok you are not working right now, but no-one is expecting me to beat myself up about it every day. That is my choice and my choice only. Attitude is everything."

The childhood song entered her head and made her smile. "When I feel afraid, I hold my head erect, and whistle a happy tune, so no-one will suspect, I'm afraid."

The band began to play and everyone clapped. Children holding helium balloons stretched taut to the sky, took their places at the table whilst the parents began to fiddle with the teddy's parachutes. The entertainer blew bubbles over the crowds that burst with wet splatters on made up faces and began to curl newly straightened hair.

The older generation tea party began with the tea dance. Bored with 70 plus years of the same style food, the pensioners were happier to neck their welcome sherry and join the "dancefloor" while they were still able.

Some of the mothers looked on with admiration, wondering if there would be happy house warehouse raves for them to go to when they were old, with an ecstasy pill to neck instead of the sherry and tea dance, or perhaps with the sherry…

The midday bells chimed above the party and the pub and shop could sell chilled beers, wine and cider and then the atmosphere became more jovial and convivial.

Everyone clapped politely, watching hungrily as the children delightedly attacked the piles of sandwiches, crisps, home grown tomatoes and home baked fairy cakes. The tapas, whilst delicious, was not a patch on children's party food and every mother with a child under 10 were still very aware of the fact and tried hard to resist popping hula hoops on their fingers.

Phelps led poor Grumph round and round the lane, covered in shouting delighted children. He was a particularly cute miniature Shetland, with a pretty strawberry roan coat that dissolved into a white face with big unusual blue eyes.

Grumph behaved brilliantly for a whole hour, but the noise of the children and the smell of cucumber sandwiches was all too much. As soon as one sweet flower haired girl slipped off, he made off for the abandoned trellis tables, barging through groups of startled children and dropped ice creams, pulling poor Jane behind him. Skidding to a halt, he opened his mouth to bare all his teeth, to the frantic screams around him and dived into the pile of untouched sandwiches. Just for final effect, he lifted his tail and dropped a pile of green wet dung behind him.

Grumph finally pulled his head away from the table to swing green foam across his admirers.

Time to go back to the field.

With a round of applause and a spring in his step, Grumph was captured and led away from the scene of devastation.

At last, it was time for the teddies from the church. To wild applause, Willy pulled off his shirt and ran up and down the steeple steps carrying boxes of parachute-bedecked teddies above his head. He laid a target point on the floor and stated that anyone whose Teddy entered the target would get a prize.

Some of the local helicopter pilots cursed their more innovative parachutes, realising that to reach the target a death plummet would be more successful than a gentle float on the breeze.

It is amazing how ridiculously funny it is to watch teddies plummet from a church tower. Phelps made a great commentator, remarking on the different teddies, such as lilac "My Little Ponies" and "Tiggers" that bounced short of the target and were quickly gathered up by their owners.

The crowd cheered wildly and Helen found a lightness in her heart. Simple game. Simple stuff could be so much more fun than being bogged down in the clever stuff all day. How she loved living here.

Jane grinned, really pleased that everyone was having fun and that so far everything was going smoothly. She caught a glimpse of Clara walking unsteadily out from the pub to watch the spectacle, her lips painted crimson and her eyebrows drawn on high in the pursuit of youth, resulting in an expression of surprise.

What a turn up, Clara might even smile!

Everyone returned to the street to help tidy up the lines of tables and reset them for the evening. The band played a range of old classics and new versions of pop songs you would think impossible to play with real instruments. Everyone cheered, buoyed up by each other's exuberance and their mid- morning drinking, they joined the pensioners in their tea dance.

The combines and tractors decided to undertake an unscheduled drive past.

A cross between a flash mob and the Red Arrows. Everyone cheered as the huge machines lumbered by at the start of the road closure, waving and flashing their powerful blinding lights as they went. A quad flew past with the young farm girl Sophie standing in the seat and waving. Of course, this was what the party was traditionally for; to celebrate the end of the wheat and barley harvest but no one except the farmers had planned this bit.

A huge roar erupted from the crowd and pints were held up in honour of the custodians of the land.

Jane slipped a call to the local press and was instructed to start taking photos.

Gervais was thinking the same. He hadn't completely given up of his idea of filming his year in the village. Wasn't there a book called "Year in Provence"? What about the "The Year after those floods?" He spoke quickly into his Dictaphone app and took film shots and photos. What a glorious day and the grown-up bit hadn't even started yet!

Everyone started to set up the tables across the road, for the evening and then went home to freshen- up. All except Clara who was up, about and onto her third bottle of wine already. John took his time to clean the bar and ensure the curry was at the correct temperature, restock the toilets.

The café shut down and cleared away and the shop did the same. Alcohol could be purchased from the shop if you asked Jane throughout the evening and she was prepared with a bucket full of ice by her table.

Seven pm came and the tables began to fill with a range of flowers and white tablecloths, wine coolers and salads, that or cans of beer and cider. The organisers sat together on a long trestle table that they had covered in tea lights and flowers. Smaller tables grouped pairs of families, the small school joined several tables together and the children darted between them to the front to dance and back again. The footballers and their girlfriends packed another long trestle table, filled with ashtrays, cans and crisps.

The first band, "The Mangle Wurzels" began to play and a scattering of people got up to dance. It started with those easy to dance to rock classics that everybody knows. Food and drinks were cracked into and the tables began to get a little louder as people relaxed.

Then the Wurzels covers began. "Combine 'Arvester" and "Black Bird I'll 'ave ee!" rattled through the valley and people began to sway with their pints.

Shane was then up with his wheelbarrow race. The evening sun was kind and shone warm, glinting off the golden walls and giving the evening a soft golden hue. Everyone lined up with customised wheelbarrows, some with the Union Jack, others dressed as tractors and some with references to the recent news items. Everyone roared with laughter as Sophie from "Home Farm" arrived in the quad with a scoop attachment and was promptly excluded.

Gervais and Tamsin sat with Tom and Estella and roared with laughter as the scurry began. Three times round the block of the centre of the village with a bucket of water. The first one back with more than ¾ of the bucket full, would win a barrel of cider – to be shared with the rest of the village of course. Immediately several of the wheelbarrows overturned and the buckets spilt across the road. Willy set the pace and stopped to strip to the waist to the cheers of the crowd. He was closely followed by one of the footballers who was cheered on by the young girls of the village. Old Jim was in the background moving slowly and everyone whistled and urged him on. Phelps was looking a little too serious as he started to manoeuvre between those at the rear and started to gain on Willy. Was it a test of youth over skill? The crowd roared again at the testosterone as the two ran with the buckets rocking precariously in the wheel barrows. Shane took up the commentary. "Come on girls look at the beef cake on offer here. Who could possibly win? Who are we gonna cheer for? Scream if you want them to go faster!" And the crowd did!

Suddenly a late contender joined the race, it was Sophie back from parking the quad. The crowd started to recite "Put 'em to shame Sophie!, Sophie, Sophie!"

She expertly wheeled the wheelbarrow, tipping sideways to master the corners without spilling a drop. Years of mucking out the horses and other livestock on the farm had trained her well and soon she was neck and neck with Phelps and Willy. All three drew to the line at the same time to the rapture of the crowd. They joined hands and passed the finishing line together, shortly followed by Jason the footballer. Jim joined on behind to more applause.

The barrel was opened and everyone came up for a taste of the winnings. Several pints being poured over the contestants at the same time.

Clara watched from the pub steps. Her face was blank and her body seemed to move without anyone at the helm. She continued to drink and take in the proceedings without joining in.

A blast of Asian fusion music began and Sarah came up on the steps.

"Your turn everyone!" She yelled

Everyone staggered to their feet and began to swing their hips and wave their hands in the air as the Zumba started.

Helen laughed and joined in. She had been sitting with Jane and Phelps but now the village were moving as one and everyone joined everyone else. There seemed to be no barriers of age or class, everyone knew everyone and everyone danced with everyone. It is amazing how dancing brings people together, especially when you don't have to worry about your creativity, just follow the leader and watch everyone gets tangled up and fall over each other. The more the merrier.

Helen's miserable existence seemed to float away and the crowd danced as one happy team, revelling in the community of the village.

Gervais and Tamsin were up joining in and no one noticed whether the two stars were good at dancing, whether they looked pretty or kept time. Tamsin felt some hands move around her waist so she wiggled accordingly and was rather bemused to see that Gervais was ahead of her laughing with Estella. Turning around, she saw Phelps behind her. Confused by the merriment of the moment he drew in to kiss he neck. She pulled away quickly, gave him gentle pat on the head.

"Oi cheeky, don't let the drink make you do something you regret."

"Oh God, sorry! Don't know what came over me!" Phelps blushed wildly. He really didn't know. He had been caught up in the cider-fuelled moment and just for a moment forgot that his fantasies were not reality.

"Oh Shit! Oh no!"

Tamsin laughed. "You've been at the winner's cider! Bad man!"

She carried on dancing and dismissed the moment. In fact, she was rather impressed by his embarrassment. It had always disappointed her, the number of married men who would approach her. It rather reinforced her approach to men and life. Use and don't get too tangled up in love. Nevertheless, apart from that quiet reminder to her subconscious, the night continued as if nothing had happened.

Phelps however was devastated by his behaviour. What was he thinking, in public, in view of his wife! What had come over him? Was it the cider, the Tamsin lust or Oh God was it a mid-life crisis?

Would he soon be dressing in red lycra and going out for hours on a racing bike? Heavens no!

What would Tamsin do? Would she tell Gervais, or please God not Jane!

He walked away rubbing his eyes as if he could gouge the scene out of his head.

Helen caught up with him. "Not so fast big man!" Gervais is about to play and you are not going to miss that!

Gervais wobbled onto the raised pavement in front of the pub, tripping over his guitar on the way. "See I can make you laugh already!"

All faces were turned expectantly watching. The crowd cheered him on. Nerves shot through him and his hands began to shake. "Please God make this go ok."

"Good evening Norton Beauchamp!" He yelled at the crowd. "Wow what a party! You lot are amazing! This beats Wembley".

He picked up his guitar and "Thank the Lord" his fingers began to remember the weeks of intensive practice they had received. His share of the winner's cider was beginning to kick in and Gervais started to move on autopilot.

"Let's start with our old favourite, you know, the one with a number and no name" He launched into a hard rock classic that had people jumping up and down and pumping the air with their fists. He then slowed it down to moan about the rain. "It's not raining on Norton Beauchamp tonight!" He yelled and then moved to one about supermarket shopping and one about insects.

He sung as he had not sung in years and thoroughly enjoyed it. His throat was killing him and he was exhausted. Sweat flung outwards like a dog shaking after a bath and the crowd jumped with him. Finally, he decided to close on a slowy and he called Tamsin up to duet a soft love song. Couples joined to each other and danced arm in arm.

"It isn't goodbye Norton Beauchamp, it isn't good night, because I still have more cider to drink and we have all these tables to put away!

He flung his hands over the strings again and played rousing themes to put tables away to.

The crowd cheered and then did as they were told, picking up the rubbish and folding the tables, swearing as they nipped their fingers in the hinges.

Then the trouble started.

Clara began to shout.

"Yes, you had better clean up this mess. You stinking scabs. How many of you bought something in my pub hey? How many times did you use the toilets and not repay us by buying our drinks? Shame on you all! Well don't expect me to come and clear up your mess, you selfish animals."

She began to scream in a strange, throaty sound. Her arms began to flail and she began to lash out at anyone near her. John rushed over and held her from behind, steadying her with his body. It was not enough for the power of drunken angst. Clara whipped around and punched him in the face, sending him staggering backwards. Everyone gasped and she swung around and marched in muttering to herself.

"Leave her!" "I can only apologise for her words. Let's just say her view is not that of the manager of the pub who loves you all and hopes that you had a fantastic time."

Helen and Jane rushed to his aid and took him inside to empty the ice bucket onto his cheek.

The villagers raised their eyebrows.

"Good old Claaara, 'er can be relied on to ruin a good aaatmosphere!" Said Shane. " John'll be all right in there with Captain Phelps and Jane. Let's help out by getting this street clean and this party finished!"

Everyone piled up the wheelbarrows with folding chairs and took them back to the village hall, followed by the tables. Litter was sorted, bagged and shared out amongst the villagers to put in their recycling and black bins.

"At least I won't be embarrassed putting out my recycling on Monday!" quipped Tom. I can blame it on you lot and not my own consumption for once!"

"Nice end to the party by the way Gervais, get us all drunkenly singing so we can get this lot put away quickly and happily."

The evening finished with everyone singing along to famous tracks, the tidying was complete and people staggered off back to their beds.

Chapter 11

The rain fell harder than it had all summer. It was almost as if it had held off until the wheat had been harvested and now it could relax.

The spring in Tamsin's kitchen thundered with the ferocity of the Niagara Falls, shouting incessantly, clattering with anger against the Belfast sink below.

Tamsin didn't hear, nor did Gervais as they slept until 11am sprawled over the bed. Tamsin staining the sheets with last night's mascara and Gervais still in his trousers, stinking after the night's excesses.

Nobody else stirred either. Most of the children had exhausted themselves and allowed their parents an extra hour lie in, not demanding entertainment and breakfast until after 7am. The hens let themselves out of the autopen; cats went out in search of breakfast whilst dogs held onto their bladders and began to whine.

Phelps woke with a dark, dirty, guilty feeling in his stomach. He lay with his eyes open, listening to the rain hitting the stable roof, remembering what he had done. He reached over and held Jane, compulsively hanging on lest she should have found out and left him. He had no energy to move and his head reminded him that any movement should be taken with care.

Thank God Betsy and Grumph were out all night. They had shelter in the field if they needed it, so there were no immediate demands. Until Aga came snuffling up, licking his hand and whining.

Phelps hauled himself out of bed, flopped downstairs and opened the back door. Aga bounced out barking. Phelps ignored him and went back to bed.

Helen shifted in her bed, awoken by the movements of the morning through her open window. She lay listening to the rain rhythmically hammering. She smiled, "Nothing to get up for." Pootle had a dog flap and last night's table left overs to keep him busy. She stretched luxuriantly over the bed, feeling the crisp sheets, cool and stiff against her skin. She turned her pillow to the cool side and closed her eyes.

Estella and Tom woke in a tangle of love making sheets. Estella slid her arm over Tom and finding his body warm and responsive, lay her body over his and began to tease her nipples over his chest and lips. Still asleep Tom responded by opening his mouth over nipples until he found them becoming hard and erect. Doing the same, he pulled her down onto him and slid in, enjoying the damp warmth of her inside. They lay together, gently licking and moving until both tensed and shuddered and fell asleep until lunchtime.

Shane went for an early walk to clear his head. He left his tarpaulin-strewn driveway and wandered towards the party site in the hopes that someone may have dropped some hard cash on the way. He collected a couple of broken bottles and several 5p coins but was not greatly richer.

He looked up at the pub and wondered how John was today. He was going to have to sort Clara out before she destroyed that pub.

Shane grinned as he recalled that had managed a smooch with one of the single mums and hoped that might develop into something if he was lucky. It had been a long time since he had fallen out with the love of his life at the time, back when the great unwashed was the fashion. She had travelled off with a crusty band member and lived off his royalties on the levels somewhere. He had been left renting an ex-council house that hadn't been renovated in years.

He wondered if Helen was up for anything, she seemed much prettier and much more alive recently. He didn't know why, but she had lost that dour expression and seemed much more welcoming of the world.

John was having horrid dreams where he couldn't see. He was staggering around the pub, unable to locate where he was until tripping against the bar. Try as hard as he could, his eyes would not open. He began to shout. Suddenly, as if an electric cattle prod had been stabbed into his heart, he leapt awake. But he still couldn't see. Trying to force his eyes open, he felt a tearing as dried blood split from his lashes and gave up their seal. They still only opened slightly and out of the crack, he could see his wife lying in the bathroom across the floor with one of the footballer's trophies by her side. Touching his eye gently, he could feel the puffiness. He groaned, there would be no pub opening today.

He went into the bathroom carefully not to wake Clara, he didn't want to have to deal with that yet, and he managed to warm bathe his eyes apart. Once clean, he realised that the swelling was not too bad, a cut from the forehead had run into his eyes and stuck them together.

He poured himself a lemon squash, refreshing for that birdcage mouth, and thumped back onto the bed with an ice pack and started to piece together the evening events.

Clara had watched Jane tending John's head from the back of the bar. When Jane and Helen had gone, she leapt out making that strange throaty noise again.

"I know you, you philanderer, I saw the way you were looking at her, all soft eyes, you never look at me that way."

She had chased him around the bar swinging a bar stool with gargantuan strength, fortified by the amount of alcohol she had imbibed. He had ducked as she swung the stool over the dirty glass pile and shattered them over the floor. John had groaned at the expense and time it would take to sort it all out. He had escaped and run upstairs. He last remembered a flash of silver above his head.

He tenderly felt again at the cut and wondered which football trophy it was. "Man of the match" would not have caused so much damage as the huge "South West Pub League Championship".

He fell back against the pillow, now noticing the crusty red layer. Thumping it over he fell asleep wondering how he was ever going to sort things out.

Chapter 12

Jane opened the new local paper and smiled at her photos of Gervais looking a mess on the steps in front of the pub.

Drunken popstar creates crowds!

Norton Beauchamp were treated to an unexpected blast from the past when drunken star Gervais James literally fell onto the stage at their annual post-harvest party and treated the crowd to a performance of his old tracks!

Formally, from 90's band "Squelch", Gervais and his beautiful ex-model wife Tamsin have settled to the country life. Living in the old Manor Farm since May, we are yet to see how Gervais is planning to use the farm to supplement his income, which at the present is based solely on royalties.

Having failed to make a huge impact on the farming world so far, is it be a better avenue for him to make money?

Is Gervais a hit or a flop in the countryside?

How do our local people think we can help Gervais make his farm work so he doesn't have to return to the stage? Readers write in, we could make it a weekly article!

Jane smiled and enjoyed the hint that Gervais may be a little incompetent. "Set the thought in people's minds and then they won't take him seriously if he tries something!"

Helen had two major appointments in her diary. Seeing the NUT advisor and her Head to discuss the future and her cognitive behavioural therapy courtesy of the NHS. She did not know which made her feel sicker.

When Helen did not think of work, or the future, she was ok. She felt calm, even more alive and rested that she had in forever. But as soon as she was made the face up to the fact she had unfinished business and an income to sort out, her stomach would rise into her throat, her teeth would clench and she would start to go dizzy, her eyesight blurred and stabbing pains and light flashes would shoot through her head and eyes. If the source of stress was taken away, the nasty symptoms go away. Couldn't she just win the lottery so that she didn't have to face up to her future? Then she could learn how to be a horse whisperer and have stables full of horses and live happily ever after.

She sighed as she looked at the dates in her diary again. Next month she would have to meet up with her head and the NUT officer to thrash out a leaving settlement. Her stomach turned again and she rushed for the bathroom.

Ok so teachers have loads of transferrable skills, but what should she commit to? A simple low paid job until her confidence returned? Starting a new career, which would mean study and not enough money to run the house? Could she return to teaching? The latter made her stomach turn over again in that deep nauseous way. Not an option.

She looked at the rain drumming on the windows again and then at Pootle. Luckily, Pootle was not a fan of the rain either, happy to run out, do her business and flop back in front of the TV. Helen looked at the wood burner and wondered if a fire in August was too decadent. Old houses with small windows and flag stone floors do get cold easily, but could she afford the wood?

Instead she began to clean away her problems, warming herself up in the process. She took a cloth and some vinegar hot water and begun on the windows.

"Mum, I am making up for the state of them when we were little." She explained. Small lead lined windows are a nightmare to buff. Perhaps she should sell up and move to a modern estate house. Still if she did that, she would have no view to make it worth cleaning the larger windows.

Cognitive Behaviour Therapy teamed with the introduction of mindfulness was the decision made about her therapy. Learning to retrain her brain so that panic was not her over riding emotion. Follow that with learning how to let the brain calm and noting the beauty of life instead of crashing through it, thinking "What if?" or perhaps, "Got to get this done so I can do the next job."

Mica her therapist was a tall, gentle dark character, Spanish or Portuguese, perhaps, Helen mused. His quick, heavy, monotone accent was sometimes hard to follow and he repeated the same phrases over and over which made her sessions a struggle sometimes. She would come home and sleep on the sofa afterwards, with Pootle curled with his nose in his tail next to her.

"So, what is it that you really like in life?" Mica asked. "What makes you feel calm and safe and happy. Where do you like to be best, do you know?"

Helen smiled. "Outside" she responded, "out walking on the hills all alone, well with the dog. Listening to the buzzard cry, the lark sing, the breeze on my face. Watching the dog snuffle for rabbits. The weather doesn't matter, well heavy rain is a pig, but tramping through mud is as meaningful as when it is dusty. In fact, I like the way that the drove goes from sludge to dust over the year."

"I can tell that you really love it," responded Mica, "Look at the way you are now leaning forward to tell me more. Your eyes have brightened and your face has relaxed. Now tell me more. On your walks, do you stop and stare or do you stomp along as fast as you can so you can get back to the computer and your planning? I want you to go outside every day. I don't care if you are walking, or gardening or perhaps if you go out and visit someone locally. I want you to stop for 2 minutes to begin with and then take it up to 3 minutes and to 4 minutes and maybe much longer. I want you to soak in these good feelings. Then practice that breathing I showed you. Fill up your lungs and your heart with the beauty of where you are. Take your time to look at those special things and allow your brain to stop thinking about every day humdrum stuff. Push out that mind babble and focus on one point, keep breathing and you will start to relax."

"Now that is it for today. Next week I want you to tell me how you got on with emptying your mind of all the babble and concentrating on those things that you love so much."

Helen left the local hospital with her sick note signed for another month and took a deep breath. She was tired, but she also knew there were some beautiful footpaths behind the small health centre and she could combine taking Pootle and to practice what she had been told. Pootle leaped at the chance for some new sniffing and bounced ahead, her tail wagging and her tongue lolling.

Helen revelled in feeling her heart beat faster and her body warm as she strode up the hill, in her mac zipped up to stop the rain. She listened to the pattering on her hood and enjoyed its rhythm. She watched Pootle stop and sniff, then gamble ahead again, and smiled. Life was very beautiful, but that didn't take away from the fact that she still was in hot water, with no job. Mica would say that fear is not real, but just an emotional response to her changing situation. Be in control of your thoughts, when they start to bubble up, tell them where to go!

But she still had to work out what the future held. Yes, she could be less scared and try to see it as an opportunity rather than a stress, but she still had no idea what to do.

"Dad, Mum, please tell me what to do." Helen implored, looking up towards the sky.

She needed the calm gentle support of the Phelps.

Jane and Steve were very pleased to see Helen. The rain had kept all of them from their usual duties. Everyone stayed in their houses, watching TV or Facebooking each other to moan about the rain. They scurried from house to car, to work, to car and back. The shop was quiet, the ground saturated, the roads and lanes turned into streams and the villagers in the flood prone areas such as Muchelney and the roads to Martock were twitching with worry and dragging out the sand bags. Horses instead of being rugged against the flies resembling Afghanistani ladies in bhurkas, looked more like a Victorian fisherman in sowesters.

Curled up on the Phelps' antique leather sofa, a left over from the Henderson's house when they decorated, sipping filter coffee, Helen relaxed. Sometimes, just having someone looking after her made things feel so much better. A simple coffee meant the earth. "Make me lunch" she willed in her head.

"I could really do with some help still with Betsy the Nutter." Phelps was saying. "You are a dream with her. How much would a whispering course cost? Is it viable? Could you supply teach and work with horses on the side?" How old are you? Does that qualify for a Prince's Trust award?"

"Take your time." Jane was following. "Pick up some simple work, pub work perhaps until you know what you want to do. Perhaps a job will come up that you are already qualified for and so you don't need to waste time qualifying again. Let's work out what you need to live on and then go from there. Is it worth selling the house? I know you love it, but perhaps there is a cheaper way. Your parents would never want it to be a millstone around your neck. It isn't manageable for one person, is it? What about getting you on one of those dating sites, Kindling isn't it? Get you a rich man and solve all the problems!

By the way, do you fancy some lunch, it isn't much, some ham left over from the shop and some home baked bread and home grown tomatoes?"

Helen felt like someone had lifted the weight from her shoulders.

Helen walked home during a slight reprieve from the rain, feeling refreshed, supported and a whole lot better. "It isn't cognitive behavioural therapy I need, she concluded, just a family to support me."

Helen began to pop over to see the Phelps every other day. She would pop into the shop for a chat with Jane and then spend time with Steve, working on Nutter. They all got on so well. Jane enjoyed supporting her like the child she never had, and Helen loved the warmth and kindness she received. After feeling so lonely and lost, it was like receiving one of those super new prosthetic legs after losing one's own.

Not quite the same as you had before, but in some ways even better than the real thing.

Nutter responded to the calm and mindfulness that Helen practiced for both herself and Nutter. She made Nutter work, focussing her mind so that she did not have time to prance and cavort. Nutter began to strengthen her neck, arching it in and using her hind legs instead of flattening her neck and taking the bit in her teeth. With competent caring hands, she began to feel safe and enjoyed being taken out. Helen started jumping her, keeping her paces small and springy, using energy and control. Before long Nutter returned to her real name Betsy.

Even the deafening military craft swooping overhead intent on finessing their flights before "Yeovilton Air day" did not cause Betsy to crash about and foam at the bit.

Betsy began to love Helen and so did Phelps.

He didn't think much of it at first. He just enjoyed her company and enjoyed watching and learning what she did with Nutter. He still thought of her as a child, the one that he had taught to shoot in the past. Nevertheless, as Helen began to develop tone and glow, Phelps began to develop deep feelings for her. He began to realise how much he enjoyed watching the motion of her hips in the saddle as she made his uncontrollable horse respond with grace and agility. He found her company easy and lively, a change from the steady Jane who normally had her head in the order and account books of the shop in the evenings.

After recovering from his close shave with Tamsin, Phelps wanted nothing of the same to happen again. He had a respect and closeness to his wife that he didn't want to compromise. It had taken him weeks to get over his near unfaithfulness. Tamsin didn't seem to have taken umbrage. She continued to behave in the usual sparkly bright manner with him and certainly didn't avoid him. Phelps was panicking that Gervais would come after him with the guitar or a platinum disc to whack him over the head. But as time drew on, his worries ceased. Almost grudgingly, he accepted that he had made no effect on Tamsin whatsoever. Good for real life, not so good for his masculine ego.

Phelps tried to allow Helen to go out on her own with Betsy and not to accompany her. He focussed back on his game keeping, preparing the land; cutting back undergrowth to reveal the paths, checking the livestock had grown over the summer and was ready to face its death.

When an old friend had a nasty fall and asked Phelps to look after his old hunter, Phelps thought nothing of it. But of course, that was how all things start.

Riding out with Helen was fun. They chatted, raced, observed the changing season and got thoroughly muddy. Together they dragged old trees and crates to build cross country fences. There were no autumn blues here.

One day as they galloped together over the slippery ground, the new hunter took a slide. His legs went out from under him and he collapsed to the ground with a grunt. Helen stayed in the saddle, but the Hunter rolled onto his side trapping Helen beneath him. Phelps's heart went into his mouth. He was off, leaping over to Helen as the Hunter staggered up and shook himself and begun to graze. Twisting the reins and throwing them under the stirrup to prevent the horses breaking their necks on them, he ran to where Helen lay in a heap.

"Helen, Helen are you ok?" He quickly did his ABC, checking she was breathing" No No No! He cried. Groggily, Helen raised her head.

"God, he winded me! Am I alright?" Helen did a quick check and slowly got up.

"Oh God Helen! I was so worried!" Phelps pulled her towards him and kissed her tenderly and deeply.

"Oh God, Sorry Helen! Um panic, I don't know what came over me. I am sorry. Scratch that, pretend that didn't happen, shock, you know, does silly things."

Tears began to fall down Helen's face. It was like betrayal. She had found a family and now in one swift move, Phelps had taken it away.

They rode home silently.

Chapter 13

The Hendersons decided to go away to beat the summer rain. Late August could be the most depressing month. It could be the most beautiful, with golden fields and warm evenings, but when it rained, you were left with just thoughts of what could be.

It nearly always rained in August. At least it had waited until half way through August to rain this year and it was always sunny in September, taunting the children as they put on their new school uniforms.

August for the Hendersons was improved by a last minute booking to Malaga. Everyone else became more depressed.

Tamsin sludged out to the chickens in her new mucker boots, wondering if countryside bliss was all it was meant to be. She had given up straightening her hair and just wore it pulled back to reveal her roots to the world.

The spring bubbled ferociously, crashing into the Belfast sink below. Tamsin wondered about bottling it. More than that, she wondered about diverting it, because it was noisy and spread cold across the stone-floored kitchen. "Romany's Bubble" she said aloud, "What can I do with you? Do you fancy falling outside the house for a while? I can get you a nice pipe? She laughed as the spring seemed to rush harder in rage. "Don't worry, I won't, maybe I can insulate the door and heat the floor".

She held her hand under it until it numbed with the cold. She wondered how long the spring had been active and pictured her predecessors collecting water, delighted they had their own spring instead of having to walk to the village well. "It took her mind back to the curse and wondered if there was such a thing as magic and gypsy spells. She began to muse about what may happen to Gervais if he did dig up the land. She began the wives common fantasy of what to do if the husband dies.

Her thoughts drifted to people in the village and wondered who would be a suitable suiter. She reckoned she could manage a rich farmer now; she had quite got into the countryside. Then she shuddered at the thought of all the farm labourers walking through her beautiful country kitchen in muddy boots.

Now that the house was straight, she was beginning to get rather bored. She needed to do more. Perhaps she could start some needlework, except everyone had tapped into the modern vintage, crafty, make it yourself trend and she knew she was not that good.

Perhaps she could do more with the farm, she didn't really like the sheep because they were smelly, but what about converting the old barn into a cottage to rent out in the summer? Farmyard country holidays could be a bit of an earner.

Gervais had become a bit of a sheep bore, learning how to graze sheep on the best land in September to increase their fertility before covering in October. He had been rather disappointed by the value that he had for their fleeces and was wondering if he could revitalise the market for rugs by the fire. He was rather hoping that Tamsin had considered making artisan rugs or other sheepskin products. He kept dropping hints but so far, Tamsin had not noticed them.

"We need a life plan". He thought to himself. He would cook dinner, have a brain storming session followed by a drinking session and see if he could get Tamsin both on his thought path and pregnant all in one night.

One thing Gervais was good at, was wooing the ladies. He popped out to the local fishmongers in South Petherton and bought scallops and prawns and calamari. He went to the bakers for sour dough rolls and then to the vegetable shop for locally grown courgettes, rocket and broad beans. "I should be growing these and selling them to the shop myself." he grumbled as he paid the price of organic locally sourced produce.

It is so lovely to buy from small locally sourced producers but it comes at a premium. Village retailers have a reduced footfall and cannot hope to compete with the supermarket prices. Local people often are struggling with the fact they have to earn ten times their average salary to buy the average house in

South Somerset villages, six to eight times in the local towns. Lucky there are so many people moving from London who can afford it!

An idea began to develop in Gervais's mind. A homegrown farm shop in those rotten stables. Sell the eggs; grow rocket, asparagus, and other expensive organic vegetables. Willy would help him set it up no doubt and Tamsin could grace it. Adverts in the local press and the Somerset magazine would do the trick. People would certainly flock to see Tamsin. Perhaps they could press their own apple juice too.

He hopped in the SUV with a lighter stride and sped home, narrowly missing a disgruntled Phelps on his horse on the way. "Sorry Phelps!" he shouted. Bloody city drivers I know!

Gervais swung into the kitchen, taking a moment to admire the new wooden surfaces Tamsin had created. He lit the aga, hoping a little extra evening warmth may have the desired effect. Prosecco into the fridge, mint chopped and added to the salad, seafood prepared and ready to go. Best undies on and spray to the slightly more muscular chest and here we go!

Tamsin slopped in with the eggs and lifted her nose to the air.

"Someone or something smells good!" Gervais was not sure if that was himself or the bread warming in the oven. He pressed on regardless.

"We are having a business meeting tonight. Get on your city slicker dress and get your sexy arse down here, dinner is served in the newly refurbished dining room in exactly 20 minutes."

Tamsin mentally cancelled her Pilate's session and went upstairs to put on her push up bra, jacket, skirt, stilettoes and a splash of fragrance. "Perhaps he will enjoy my idea about the holiday home," she considered as she realised that her bra was getting tighter and her waistband harder to reach. "Countryside is rather good for you." She mused, thinking she had better cut out the second glass of wine a night.

Pulling her hair high to emphasise her long neck, she wondered what Gervais had in store for her tonight.

After a bottle of prosecco and seafood, Gervais was beginning to lose his thread and become increasingly obsessed with the shape of Tamsin's perfectly curved breasts.

"So, if I can have another ten thousand, I reckon I can have that house ready for guests," Tamsin was saying. "If it doesn't work we can sell it and make a pretty penny."

"Well, I think we should get Willy to help us with getting vegetable beds ready for next spring," Gervais said. "You would look great in a pinny."

"Let's go out and look at the space we have got," Suggested Tamsin coquettishly. "And bring the other prosecco bottle with you."

As they strolled out into the evening calm, Tamsin lifted her nipples to the top of her bra and put on her best business face.

"So, this stable here would make a lovely two bed apartment, see? Look, the walls are strong and the floor can be renovated. A bit of plaster work is required, that's all."

"I suppose we could build a shed for our vegetable shop I suppose, a lean to, or use the side or the other barn." Gervais was watching his plan unravelling in front of his wife's nipples.

"Shall we go upstairs to where the fleeces are stored and look at what we could do with those?" Gervais suggested suggestively.

"So, you think the holiday home is a god idea then and I can have the money?"

"Oh, you're gorgeous; I'll do anything for you. I will go to the bank tomorrow. I promise"

They bounced onto the washed fleeces and became lost in the idea of milkmaids and young masters in the barns of old, strangely twisted into business suits and modern day.

A slightly diminished Gervais went to the bank manager the following morning to discuss converting into a holiday home.

"So, what have you discovered about your development plans?" Asked the manager." You were planning on developing that land, remember the one with covenant that wasn't a covenant?"

Gervais came home with the holiday home money agreed and a revived interest in his initial grand plan.

"Right we are going to get an architect round to look at the site and make a decision." Gervais stated to Tamsin the following evening after googling the process.

"Have you thought about the curse and the covenant that the villagers talk about? You are not going to make us very popular, can you live here knowing everyone hates you?" Tamsin responded. "What about if I go and find out more about this. I wonder if there is any information on the internet, perhaps I could go to Taunton museum or maybe chat to some of the older people in the area and know what it is all about."

"There is no covenant, and how can there be a curse? What clap trap!"

Chapter 14

"Bastard, bastard bastard!" Helen could not get Phelps's kiss out of her mind. Why couldn't her just behave himself? "God knows I'm not totally irresistible!" She mentally compared her own short riding fit muscular legs against Tamsin's slim armpit high pins.

He had ruined everything. She couldn't go near him now. Ok he had tried to apologise when he was rebuked, but that was probably more to save face, than because he had made a mistake.

"What do I do now?" already Helen was missing his company and Jane's. She wondered what Jane must be thinking about her sudden non-appearance.

"What did I do to make him even think I would have an affair with him and ruin Jane's life." God its' not fair, I hate men and their stupid cock led brains."

Trouble was Helen had seen the love in his eyes and for a fleeting second, felt the warmth and comfort of someone strong holding her and she wasn't entirely sure that she could trust herself now.

Phelps took his anger out on the rusty barbed wire fence that he found in twisted in his hedges.

"Stupid stupid bastard, what have I done? What if she tells Jane? What about poor Betsy?" Phelps remembered the words of his primary school teacher and for once considered them useful.

"If you make a mistake, face up to it, admit you are wrong and try to put it right. It may be embarrassing and difficult but people will respect you for it."

John was also miserable.

He looked around the tatty surrounds of the pub. "God, it needs a proper women's touch." He muttered. The carpet was stained and tattered, the bar scratched and dull. The old red velvet seats were ripped and smelly. Pam was flopped on the floor creating an odorous cloud around her.

Outside it was wet. The dull skies made it look even duller inside. John felt dull, his head was still aching from the beating it had taken, his cheek still reddened. He sighed and checked the beer, pouring a little for Pam to test.

The latch on the door lifted and John saw the swing of long chestnut hair and the patter of chocolate coloured curly footsteps.

"Helen! So good to see you!" I haven't seen much of you since you took on Phelps' horse. He seems rather miserable these days. What have you done to him?"

Helen deflected the question by ordering herself a cider.

"I have been out walking with Pootle. Still bloody raining out there. Think I deserve this!"

"Me too!" exclaimed John and poured himself a bitter. "Think I will join you. I am planning what this pub will look like when I get Clara's life insurance."

"What are you planning?" Helen settled herself for an interesting conversation.

"Well I thought I might brew some double concentrated alcohol, like that Caribbean Rum 80% volume or something. Pour it in with her usual wine and let her poison herself with alcohol. It is inevitable, that's how she will go sooner or later."

"NO!" Helen exclaimed, "What are you planning to do with the pub!"

Two hours passed in a minute as they involved themselves in ideas and plans, moving walls, choosing flooring and fabrics. No-one else came in and disturbed them and both felt in high spirits until Clara came and broke the moment.

"I'm watching you young lady. Can't get your own man, don't take mine, for what he is worth. Right seeing as it is so quiet, I am going back upstairs." She swiped a bottle of wine and clomped back up the staircase.

"Well she put a lot of effort into defending your honour!" Helen giggled and felt lighter and less strained than she had since her fall.

She had been back riding, but waited until Phelps had gone to work before working on the two horses. It had kept her busy, schooling Nutter and exercising the hunter and her worries about teaching had been pushed to the back of her mind.

She felt lonely though, not able to pop over to the Phelps, she would pop into the shop to chat to Jane, but felt a bit of a fraud, knowing the feelings she had somehow encouraged in Phelps. She missed their chatter and the humour of Phelps and although she had no romantic feelings towards him, she realised how much she needed male company in her life.

Walking back, she decided to face the mud and wet grass and walk through the valley. The sun was setting at about 8pm these days and the freshness after the rain was tempting her nostrils. She slid down the grassy slope and followed the River Bubble, swollen and brown charging noisily through the valley. Pootle leaped around shooting after rabbits and returning to check on her location every so often, panting at the exertion and thoroughly enjoying herself.

As Helen got to the bottom, she became aware of another dog shooting out of the woods. A huge hairy lurcher leaping around and chasing Pootle, barking and resting down on her front legs to tempt Pootle into play. Helen turned to look where he had come from and saw a figure moving towards her. An arm was raised in greeting and so Helen turned to say hello.

"Finally stopped raining." came a deep masculine voice with a trace of the Somerset dialect. Helen had a double take. She had obviously been watching too much Poldark on Sunday evenings because she could be sure that this long black, curly haired Adonis was striding towards *her*. He was wearing just a white t shirt and battered jeans, a modern-day version of the billowing white shirt.

Helen blinked and waited for the Poldarkian version of heaven to turn back into Willy, or one of the other locals, but it didn't seem to be happening. Perhaps, if she was lucky, she could dream up the stunning black horse that Poldark galloped across the Cornish cliffs as well.

"Is my dog worrying you?" Came the voice.

"Oh! No!" gasped Helen, her heart starting to thump in her throat in the most inconvenient manner and her cheeks feeling warmer than she would have liked.

"Which way are you walking?"

"Oh um, any way really, just stretching my legs and watching the sunset."

"Come my way if you like, I haven't talked to another human today, unless you include my old toothless Dad and that is not a mind broadening experience."

"Um. Well, yes why not? I'm Helen, I live over there in the cottage on the edge of Manor Farm Lane."

"I'm Jake Isaacs, I'm living in that caravan through the trees over there."

Helen's heart tightened. Simultaneously, she thought "Like Ross Poldark" and "Shit one of the gypsies" as she clutched her purse and phone.

Jake strode effortlessly along through the wet tangled grass and Helen had to pick up her pace. Ahead, 'Enry the lurcher bounded with the long easy strides Helen could only dream of and Pootle shot after him.

"So, what are you doing living on Gervais's land?"

"Gervais is it, what that new pop star come farmer? Well a few reasons really.

Number one, Keeping up our heritage. This is ancient gypsy land. The gypsies always stopped here with the permission of old Tom and his father before that. It was great for picking the Martock beans.

Number two, I hear that your Gervais popstar man wants to build on this land despite knowing about the covenant. Well he will find it a damn sight harder once we have squatter's rights! Stupid dolt doesn't even know we are here yet!

Ok Number three, less altruistic I am afraid, and yes, I did go to school and learn some big words on the way. We are homeless, we have been moved on and moved on. I need to get settled so the kids can get a decent education.

Helen's heart sank at the sound of children. Of course, he has probably been married since he was 16. She had watched the "fat gypsy" documentaries on TV. They were in full time business by 14 and married at 16 with their own van bought from the proceeds of the previous year's hard graft and dubious business deals.

"What about toileting and mess?" Helen had heard about the state the gypsies left their camps in.

"Well if we are given time to settle in one place, we dig a long drop compost toilet. The vans are equipped with showers and toilets, so we just use it as fertilizer, nature's way. We want to look after nature, it is our life. People do get angry though when they are thrown off land, so then they do leave a mess for the council, like a goodbye note almost! Come and have a look if you like!"

Helen was immediately entranced by the sight of a grey pony and a skewbald gypsy cobb grazing from a stake and chain. In between them was a young filly wagging her tail like a new born lamb. She wobbled over to say hello to Helen, her long bendy legs folding in the process.

"Wow so friendly!"

"We handle them from the minute they are born so they know no different. I believe love is the best way to break a horse."

"Me too, I've been studying horse whispering."

"Brill tell me more!"

The two animal lovers chatted over a cup of tea heated on the fire (there was a kettle inside but somehow that would have ruined the moment.)

Neither of them noticed how Pootle the poodle and 'Enry the brindle lurcher were getting on. 'Enry had bounded over to Pootle, lowering himself on to his forearms and bouncing up again to encourage Pootle to play. The two of them were soon shooting up and down the hills, chasing and leaping on each other and bounding away again.

Helen returned to her house as the sun was lowering and the blackbird was scolding. A smile was stretched over her face and her cheeks were hurting, but she couldn't stop it. "Mum, Dad thank you!" she whispered.

Chapter 15

Gervais was determined to get started on his building project before the harvest was over. He was hoping that while people were getting used to going back to school, getting the potatoes, maize and beans in and clutching at the last summery days to run down to Lyme Regis, he could sneak in the planning permission objections and get cracking.

He had researched and chosen a building company from out of town so that word would not get out. The architect had chosen a simple quick to build but pretty plan.

Gervais had agreed to digging as soon as the planning period was due to close so that people would assume the project had gone through. The architect was also worried about the lay of the land, with the river running through clay, would it flood, or would the land become quickly saturated and then dry in the summer causing cracks and settlement issues.

Tamsin, after winning over Gervais with her plan to build her guest house, had eventually been swayed to his ideas of selling local produce. She had started to covet books on crafty ideas and healthy cooking and was quickly working on her produce shop.

Aware there was no produce from the fields this year, she was concentrating on free range organic eggs, slaughtering the odd lamb and sheep to create fashionable cuts of meat and demonstrating her happy organic farm living. She had also opened the walls for an art gallery and was hoping that the venue could be up and running albeit in a temporary shed, for the Somerset Arts Week, so that her new venture could be known. Fused glass seemed to be popular and easy to sell, so she was hoping to gain an artist residency to adorn the windows. She had started to sell fashionable vintage paint and demonstrated interesting things to paint, displaying them on cut and painted pallets. She was also considering the idea of selling home baked produce and was considering the food handling regulations. Her creative side was really coming to the forefront and she was really enjoying it.

She was so fulfilled and busy that she wasn't really watching what Gervais was up to. In fact, she had been spending increasingly time with Willy as he took over her handy man. He was simple, jolly, flattering and cracked silly jokes that lightened the atmosphere on a day to day basis. He acted like a proper gentleman, holding the door for her, taking heavy boxes and paying her compliments. Tamsin began to feel young and special again. Slowly she found her attention was wandering away from Gervais, made content by her creativity and her young man. And that was before you consider how pretty he made the scenery.

The land surveyors came and decided to dig a deep hole to check the quality of the soil. Gervais asked for it to be larger than necessary and rather deep. "Leave it there" he said. "I want the locals to think that building is inevitable, already started so there is no point complaining. Ever heard of retrospective planning permission?"

How he underestimated the locals.

Jane was quickly informed of the goings on by Willy. "Time to up the press power!"

With the start of term, Helen had decided just to hand her notice in. She told the NUT to forget a settlement. She did not want to talk to her head or to face discussions over her ability to do her job. Whenever she thought about school, bile rose in her throat. There was no way to go back. It should have felt liberating, but she just felt a failure, embarrassed to show her face and aware that she had only two months to sort her life out before she would lose the house. The worst bit was seeing the school bus pick up the local children and the sounds of children playing in the village school playground. "I am supposed to be there. What a failure. And what am I doing instead?"

Relief at coming to the decision had helped, but with no-one to talk to, she resorted to popping into the pub to see John and have a pint of cider.

John for all his down trodden ways, could be quite funny. He was a slow observer of life. Having mucked his own up so completely by losing his self-esteem and motivation to Clara's bottle and punches, he sat and contemplated others. When people were drunk, their core personalities came out. He knew more about the village then anyone. He didn't share what he saw, that was part of the job description, but he used it to inform his own decisions and confirmation of what life was about.

He had been deciding increasingly that her was going to have to do something. His chats with Helen had brightened him and made him realise that there was still a personality within him. Still something worth saving. After all he was still in his 40's and that was his age as well as his waist size. Time for project John.

"Aaaftnoon my darlin'" He said warmly as Helen was dragged through the door by a bouncy Pootle. Delightedly, she woofed and pranced around Pam to get her to play. Pam looked up at her and ruffed a deep sound and lowered her head. Pootle gave her a lick and encouraged Pam to get up and follow her to the garden. Pootle had been seduced by the play power of 'Enry and wanted more.

"Cor if only life were as simple as tis for dogs eh? Seen any more of your young beau?"

Helen took her stool and sipped the cool amber sweet liquid. There was nothing more satisfying than sitting at the bar with a pint of cider in the summer. The rain may have been heavy, but the temperature was still warm enough for cider. She idly contemplated that Christmas was on its way and that pre-Christmas dieting should be undertaken soon. But for what and whom? She used to spend it with her family and then later with Jane and Phelps. Sometimes she would take herself on foreign exploits to mask the emptiness the season produced in the lonely. What would it be this year?

"I had a great bonny last night, did you see it? I got all the hedge trimmings that were still dry and it went up like a beacon. The flames were nearly 10 foot! Amazing considering how much it has rained. Got rid of all the pruning and burnt a few old documents as well. I can get in the office now." Helen drew from her fresh pint.

"Can't beat a good bonny, makes I feel good. Clears the rubbish and makes it fresh for the next season. Speaking of, I'm wondering about this year's fireworks display. I be thinking of 'avin one 'ere at the pub, maybe some indoor fireworks and a local band, or maybe I should set up as a sanctuary for all the scared dogs. Perhaps you could give I an 'and to make it good like."

"Well I know the village committee are planning on doing the usual outdoor display with mulled wine and food made by the school PTA. Perhaps you could have the after party? What about having a theme and dressing up. What about a theme of forks? Not Guy Fawkes, just forks? Or you could do an anti-party for all those terrified by fireworks! Could be a blast if it rains! What does Clara think?"

"Oow knows what 'er thinks. 'Er changes with which wine 'ers stolen from the cellar. No I intend to make sure 'er is well out of it by the time the party starts. Not a word to no-one yet. By the way I thinks we need another meeting about old Gervais and his naughty building plans, I'm sure I saw men with clip boards out there t'other day."

Helen forgot about her own woes and indecisions whilst she chatted to John about much more exciting topics. They were building a plan to ensure that Gervais would find it very hard to build on that ground.

A high-pitched squeal penetrated the early arriving darkness in September.

"Look at the size of those mosquito's! They're everywhere Oh My GOD Oh My GOD! We are going to die tonight, they could be carrying anything! Wait am I pregnant? What if they carry that disease that damages babies! Oh God Get rid of them!"

Some were bumping against the ceiling, others hanging upside down like a bat on a rocky precipice, the old diamond windows had become a portal for enormous mosquito like creatures and Tamsin was scared.

Not sure what else to do, Gervais rang Willy. Jim got there first and roared a throaty thunderous laugh down the line.

"They be Daddy Long Legs ye fool!" "Completely 'armless, bloody stupid things. Just shut thy window come dusk and ye'll be fine. They be gone be October."

Feeling rather silly, Tamsin and Gervais opted for a glass of red in front of the numerous showings of a TV talent show. Looking up at the high ceilings, Tamsin muttered that there seemed to be plenty of unreachable cobwebs to catch the pesky critters and then she would get them with her new cordless dyson and that would be then end to her horror.

"Have you ever been to a Somerset Carnival?" Estella asked Tamsin in early October.

"Well I have been to Notting Hill Oh and I went to the one in America, in the deep South where it got flooded. What is it called? New Orleans."

"You are almost as travelled as us. But both of those are nothing compared to Somerset. We have loads of costume and floats. The procession is the main thing, not the drinking and the dancing, though everyone does all that too, but it is more of a family thing and much more innovative.

It's been going on for as long as I can remember. All the farmers and hauliers lend their tractors and trailers and lorry flat beds. The local carnival groups dress them up with thousands of lights and thumping music that goes right through you and sets your insides leaping and your eyeballs throbbing. It is amazing! The Majorettes dance and the Brownies and Scouts dress up and create floats too. Sorry we must call them carts these days. Not sure why. People go to "Carnival" instead of "The Carnival too." There's progress and there is losing our tradition if you ask me.

Any way there is one in every major town in the area, working its way up to the biggie in Bridgwater where they do "Squibbing", a type of firework dance too.

Do you fancy coming to Ilminster with us? It is worth going with someone who knows all the places to park when they close off the roads. Ilminster one always seems to get stuck so you have to go in certain places to see it all."

"What do you mean "Stuck?"

"Have you seen the size of the streets in Ilminster? Have you seen the size of the tractors? There is always one prat who doesn't clear their parked car on the day and the procession is stuck until they can find someone to move it!"

That weekend, wearing heavy rainproof jackets, Tamsin and Gervais were astonished and delighted to throw coins at passing vehicles. They learned to step back quickly before their toes were almost squashed by tractors and lorry cabs as tall as the houses. The music thumped through their very being whilst the characters held a motionless tableau, dressed as Disney princesses, or country bumpkins and pirates, all chained onto the vehicles to prevent the unthinkable. Small children plodded the 2-mile circuit, some dancing in tiny dance outfits, others in heavy fancy dress. The sheer sensory override of bright lights, emotive music, the smell of candyfloss and frying onions along with the sheer excitement of being part of something amazing was not lost on the city couple.

"You don' t need to drink or do drugs to enjoy this carnival. You don't have to dance after ear blasting speakers and eat jerk chicken here. This is truly English and totally amazing!"

"Instead of "I sewed the sequins on myself" it is "I secured all the lightbulbs myself" and they are all eco light bulbs! That must cost a fortune!"

"Cor I must go to the fair ground and get a goldfish for the pond. And some candy floss to get stuck in my hair."

That night Gervais's ears were ringing and he couldn't help humming "Go wild, go wild, go wild in the country!" He was really enjoying leaving the over fashionable wanna be desperate stink of London and enjoying the confident careless enjoyment of the countryside.

Helen was in stress again. This time it was nothing to do with employment.

Pootle had gone missing. She had disappeared whilst on a walk and had not returned. Helen knew enough about dogs in the country to know that they usually return a few hours later with their tongues hangin out and a guilty but very happy look on their faces. She was worried that Pootle had been shot by a farmer for chasing his sheep. It would certainly be within their rights to do so. Helen soothed herself by appreciating that as Pootle was the only poodle in the area, the local farmers would give her a call before raising arms.

She decided to pull on her country boots again and set out for the valley via the pub. Just so that she could put out a message of course!

No-one had seen a thing and being too worried to enjoy her pint, Helen set it aside and prepared for the muddy lanes.

Vainly calling her name and checking the fields, Helen worked her way to the valley. Perhaps Jake would have seen her. Worth a check? Helen grinned at her own sneaky ulterior motive.

When she got there, no-one was about apart from the old man.

"Are ye looking for yur darg?" came a voice from the shiny white van.

Helen stepped up to the door to see a female face as round as the moon and crumbly as stale bread.

"I dunner know what yoor number is so I kept 'er 'ere till you found us. 'Appen I think 'er and 'enry have been enjoying time together. No don't worry, I 'aint gonna charge you boarding fees! You get on now young maid."

Patting the bi coloured gypsy cobs grazing from a chain and sharing breaths with the filly, Helen strode back up the steep sided valley with a rather unwilling and crestfallen Pootle on a lead.

Of course, he was married. Helen had conveniently forgotten in all her daydreams. And here she was, full of life.

One Tuesday night, dark at 7:30 pm the committee drew together to sort out the plan.

"So why did Old Tom's Grandfather put a covenant on the land?" Tom Henderson asked as they all ordered their pints and waved them in the direction of Clara to show they weren't taking advantage of her kind hospitality.

"Nobody knows the truth." explained Jane. It has been passed through the ages that there used to be a village along the line of the river, but the Romanies put a curse on it, hence the name. Not sure what the curse was, but the tradition has held. Apparently, it is alright for the gypsies to camp on for the harvest and for cloven hoofed animals to graze but nothing is allowed to break the surface of the earth. Perhaps the devil slips out."

It was explained that the covenant was supposed to have existed for as long as anyone could remember. Not that much had been written down in the past. Great houses like Barrington and Montacute may have contained learned men but most history was passed by word of mouth and just was common knowledge to all.

"Right then!" concluded Shane, "Sounds like Gervais needs some scaring. Who fancies creating some strange happenings around his farm. Nothing bad like, no grand chicken slaughtering. Just a presence to put the Willies up him."

"I've seen Willy over there rather a lot lately." Confirmed Helen, "Perhaps he is the passport to creating a bit of fear in the city folk!"

"What about starting with some simple moving of things. Opening of windows and repositioning of his stock. No theft of course, just strange happenings with no explanation."

"Ha ha what about getting one of those blocks to show which ewes have been covered. What are they called Raddle that's it! Cover all his sheep in it so he wakes up to a blue and red herd! Won't harm the sheep but should put the Willies up him!"

"Going back to Willy, we need to get him to do some spying and find out what we can sabotage!"

"No not sabotage, we are not going to be done for criminal damage. No just silly harmless jokes."

"We also need to remind Gervais of the curse, so he gets the idea like. What about a little article in the history of the village in the weekly newsletter and on the website?"

The brain storming continued well into the third pint and jobs were divvied up.

Chapter 16

Phelps was still missing Helen. So was his wife Jane. "Whatever you and Helen have fallen out over, I don't care, but please sort it out with her. Who else has she got poor girl. And with Christmas coming up and all. Do you want me to get some flowers delivered?"

"No, I will sort it. But thank you, I will." Phelps felt a weight lift of his shoulders. Perhaps if he apologised and explained that he got all confused, perhaps she would come around and they could get things back to normal. He had really been enjoying riding out with someone and the horses missed being together. He had got used to having her around.

He decided on a letter of apology with some flowers. He would leave them when she went out on Betsy who no longer deserved to be called Nutter.

Helen, meanwhile had not been thinking much about Phelps. She was more troubled about the fact that she had found another married man. "Please Mum, there must be someone out there for me!" She gasped exasperatedly to her passed mother.

She smiled at her own behaviour but all the same, felt a wave of peace come over her. "Don't give up"

Before she knew it, Helen had whistled Pootle, who was glad to oblige and it was time for a walk. Pootle didn't need any directing. She bounded down the hill and straight through Romany's Bubble. Helen laughed and galloped down the tussocky hill behind her.

"Coming for a walk?" She laughed breathlessly as she made it down to the collection of caravans and trucks in the settlement. 'Enry bounced out from behind a van with a small dirty faced pile of blond curls being dragged behind.

"Oh!" gasped Helen "Sweetie, are you ok?"

The child giggled and run away and then returned dragging a large, dark round, lumbering frame robed in scruffy traveller style clothes. Helen felt a surge of relief and then instantly chided herself for being uncharitable.

"Yer oow are you? Oh is it you with that poodle again from up the 'ill. What dyooo want? You after my Jake?"

"'Er sorry, no, Pootle loves 'Enry so much, she just galloped over here. Sorry to disturb you, we'll be off."

Feeling rather more deflated then she wanted to admit to, Helen trudged off and continued through the fir plantation.

"Right, pull it together, jobs time. What am I going to do?" Helen changed her point of focus.

Thoughts of horse whispering training filled her mind completely whilst she followed the steep path to the top of the hill. Could she work on teaching supply until she got on the course? Her stomach cramped and she began to feel sick. "Perhaps not!" She said aloud to the world.

A job at the pub? Will that give me enough money to survive? Would John have the money to pay me? What about a Christmas temp job to see me to January? I could be a posty, pre-Christmas fitness and pay all rolled into one!

Helen grinned and felt the energy surge back into her footsteps.

As she arrived back home her stomach lurched.

"Shit what is that by the door? Who has moved my bins, what's going on?" Pootle's nose was pinned to the ground as she zigzagged across the drive. Moving towards the door, her stomach lurched even more as she saw a huge bouquet of roses and lilies wrapped exquisitely in pink.

Jake? John? Phelps? She bent down and tore off the attached letter. She kneed open the door with her arms full and staggered into the hall whilst Pootle pushed past her.

Dear Helen,

Please accept my apologies for my misdemeanour.

I think I just got confused with my reaction. I was just so scared when you fell so badly and then so relieved to see you were ok.

You have been like the daughter that Jane and I couldn't have and I would never ever want to ruin that relationship.

We both miss you very much and I hope that you can trust me never to let anything like this happen again. You do not need to feel awkward around me or worse still be scared that something like that is a possibility.

Please, please accept my apologies and I hope that you will feel able to join us for lunch on Saturday so we can get back to the great trio that we once were.

Your friend
Phelps

Helen sat heavily on the sofa and her stomach lurched again. Her brain emptied and she just sat and did nothing. She forced herself to read the letter again. A sweep of embarrassment engulfed her and she began to perspire. She had managed to avoid thinking about it until this and now she is going to have to face up to it.

She put the letter on the side and drank a glass of water. Then she started to clean. Again, the guilt, fear and nerves were pushed into cleaning the windows and scrubbing the carpets. Two hours later with red sore hands, she sat down and faced up to it with a text thanking Phelps for the flowers and agreeing to be friends but not lunch yet. Soon.

"Willy, have you moved that stack of pallets that were around the side of the shop?" called Tamsin in October. She had been selling huge dahlias that had been planted by a local farm and wanted to make a display using an old enamel jug she had found in the back of the barn.

"Pallets? They be round the side of the shop, unless Gervais 'as moved them.

'Ere did you read in the newsletter about Halloween and how the old curse on your land is supposed to raise its ugly face. The reckon lots of poltergeist tricks start to happen with the change in the season. Used to blame it on the kids in the old days. Old Tom wouldn't let anyone on his fields once the rain had soaked it, in case it broke the surface, like the covenant says. Gypsies would be on their way in early October once the beans and potatoes were harvested and so the land was left fallow."

"What are you suggesting Willy, that the developers have woken up the curse which has moved the pallets?"

"Well it is less strange then the idea that Gervais moved 'em. Pardon me saying like, but 'e seems more interested in thic valley than what you have been achieving here. Oh meant to ask him, is 'e getting his ewes ready for tupping? Does 'e have a ram or is he going to rent one?"

"Oh, I don't know, you are right, he hasn't said anything apart from talking about building designs. I will talk to him. We do have Bertie the ram, but I know nothing about *tupping* you say? Sounds like something from Shakespeare."

"Getting your ewes ready to have lambs in the spring. This is the right time because the shorter days make the ewes more fertile. 'e needs to get them grazing that valley full of rich grass, so that they're 'ealthy and produce lots of eggs. He then straps a box of dye onto the front of the ram and puts him in with the ewes so that you can see who is pregnant."

Tamsin smiled and watched Willy as he spoke, his muscular arms gesticulating and pointing. He was about so often and she had begun to find him lots of jobs. The land looked beautiful. Well mown with neat hedges and duck ramps on to the island. The hen houses were clean and well maintained and he had begun to tidy up the front of the house and organise the orchard. He had discussed where he should dig the vegetable patch for next year's produce and was discussing the planting of brassicas to sell for the Sunday lunches and to cover the land to improve nitrogen levels.

She felt like she was living in some sort of paradise, or at least a show house and her mind started to wander over the idea of getting another magazine article. Perhaps to show off the new business, in the local freebies or the County magazine, or Home and Country?

Her next job was to find out about the spring that ran through the scullery. Could she create some sort of insulation to stop it from getting cold, or perhaps flooding in the winter? It would be impossible to just pipe it away. She had got so used to it chattering to her in the summer months. It seemed to respond to her mood as well as the weather. It seemed to guide her thoughts by clattering louder during bad ideas. Perhaps she should run the idea of a magazine visit past it and see what it thought. Perhaps the spring will know about the disappearing pallets or the supposed curse.

Neither Tamsin or Gervais were yet aware of their squatters and they were getting more legal by the minute. Jake was enjoying being close to such beautiful land. It was so much better than the edge of a main road. He had dug the long drops and built withy outdoor furniture that any boy scout would have been proud of. They were stuck into the ground and would begin to leaf in the spring, creating living sculptures.

The children were loving it. They had grown healthy skinned and energetic, chasing the dogs up and down the hills. They were enjoying managing the woodland and using the ponies to drag logs through the undergrowth to put together as huts to sleep and store in.

Jake had respected the covenant and kept the building in the forest and grazed the ponies away from the protected area. If they were settled for long enough, he would start taking the kids to pre-school. He was beginning to believe that moving here may be more of a good idea than just stopping the building. Perhaps he could really stay?

He smiled as he thought of another reason to make him want to stay.

"Time for a walk 'Enry?" he whistled and set off along the edge of the woods and up towards the village.

Pootle was barking. "What is wrong with you?" Helen gasped exasperated. She opened the door and with a whip across her legs, Pootle was off. Staggering to pull on her boots and chase after her, Helen's language was rather ripe. Sweaty and red faced, she slammed the door, double checked she had picked up her keys and strode straight out and fell over a twisting circle of legs, noses and tails.

As she gathered herself together, Helen rose and found herself lurched into soft, blackness.

"Wooah! Are ye ok?" Jake was grinning as he put his arms around her to steady them both. "Sorry Helen, 'Enry leapt up here, I wondered where she was going, must have been the lure of the lovely Pootle! Are you ok?"

Head spinning, Helen didn't make a move to extricate herself. She smiled and looked up at Jake's dark eyes and revelled in the size of his body wrapped around her.

"So this is how the other 'arf live?" Jake smiled and nodded at the hamstone cottage.

Helen's heart began to bash in her chest and throat. She smiled and aimed at a casual tone. "Come in for a coffee if you like? The dogs will be fine leaping around in the garden."

"Why not? Can I get a tour of your abode too?"

"Of course, though I haven't had the opportunity to tidy up."

Jake laughed. "Romanies may be fans of bleach and a scouring brush but we don't expect others to be as house proud as us! Put the kettle on."

Jake ducked below the door frame as he followed Helen into the dark cool of the flag stone floored kitchen. Hurling himself onto a pine carver chair, he started with the usual chit chat.

"Rain's been rather heavy. We gotta be careful not to break the land surface. Not so easy with horses. Luckily ours are all barefoot which helps. We usually tie them to a chain but I will have to invest in an electric fence as they are churning up the ground already."

Helen's interest was piqued. "Do you think there is any truth in the curse then?"

"I don't really know, but we do like to follow tradition. There is usually a good reason for it. generations of Romany learning should not be ignored by 20 years of the computer age. Most rules are for common sense, like not eating mussels in months without the letter "r" in.

Talking of the curse, I see that your pop star is pressing on with the planning. I see he has dug a big hole down there. I wonder if anything will happen."

Helen smiled. "Between you and me, I think the villagers are going to make sure that Gervais is totally spooked by the curse!"

"Ha ha, perhaps I should put some ancient patrons out. He will think they are signs from the occult."

"Patrons?"

"In the old days before phones, the gypsies would direct their friends by leaving little signs in the countryside to show the route of a gypsy caravan. Bent twigs, arrows and the like, ready for the other gypsies to follow. Perhaps I could make a little corn doll and leave it on his wall. I could even add some pins if you like! "

They both giggled conspiratorially.

"Could you show me some patrons and some other Romany craft? What about a peg and some lucky heather?"

The afternoon was whiled away with shiny straight brunette pulled close to black curls as Helen attempted ancient Romany tradition ready to spook their near neighbour and unwitting land lord.

With a light and frivolous heart, Helen admired the two corn dollies Jake had given her. He had taken another over to place in Gervais's yard by the barn. As she climbed the creaking stairs, she turned them together and wished it could be Jake and herself.

Sadly, the dollies were to have more of an immediate effect on Tamsin and her young gardener than they were for poor Helen.

The Autumn rains had continued. It usually did at this time. The farmers would just get the grains in and then it would start. The potato, carrot, beets and maize harvests would wreck the fields. Huge machinery tyres would drag the top soil onto the roads in heavy dollops. The rain would soak them thoroughly and then splatter it across your car.

All vehicles would be covered in the same sandy brown to begin with and then as the rain continued and the mess would get deeper, they would end up with dark brown splatters up to the door handles, clumps hanging off the wheel arches and covering rear windscreens until they were only visible where the windscreen wipers had struggled to clean.

There was no point washing them. Every car park and disused garage forecourt was full of enthusiastic Eastern European car washers, who would take care to produce a high standard of work. Your car would be gleaming whilst you did your shopping. Get out of the town and you would be forced into the sludge by an oncoming car and all that hard work was undone.

As a grudging nod to legality, number plates would be wiped over and then the mud would be left to build up until the cold snap came.

A positive effect of the rains was the beauty held in the Somerset Moors. The fertile grazing land around the heavily laden rivers of the Yeo, Isle and Parrett vanished as the water engulfed the land. Vast inland lakes teamed with murmurating starlings and tranquil swans. As the sun slid behind the Blackdown hills, red and golden streaks mirrored off the lakes causing dazzling bands of gold, punctuated by the black frames of unhinged gates and bent withy trees. The rhynes created slithers of silver, framed by the high banks dug each year as a barrier to further flooding.

Tamsin had been turning her energies to her own projects and she had not seen much of Gervais and his antics with the planning. She had been employing Willy on a nearly daily basis to help her sort out the undeveloped area of the barn. She enjoyed his lively banter and his tales about the naughty things that the locals seemed to get up to. Flouting planning regs, numerous affairs, gun waving retributions and struggling on benefits.

She appreciated having Willy around increasingly because the number of strange mini occurrences were on the increase and it made her feel safe having Willy around. Why things kept disappearing and turning up in the most ridiculous places was beyond her. Was she getting forgetful in her old age, did she need to become more organised in herself? But how did the pallets she had set up the night before, end up in the hen hut? The cockerel was found in the barn and the sheep had somehow changed pasture through a padlocked gate!

The spring in the kitchen was no longer a bubble. It had become a raging torrent, angrily crashing into the Belfast sink. She had asked Willy for his advice on containing it, but he didn't have much to say on the topic. Willy seemed to be focused on the strange occurrences and on discussing the curse.

On another wet Autumnal morning, the crimson leaves were being deposited around the base of the trees like a child shrugging off his dressing gown. Tamsin walked along the drive, cursing at the gravel sludge staining her damp shoes. As she got to the barn door she screamed aloud as the little face looked up at her from the floor.

"Oh my God! God! Oh no!" she screamed. "It's the Wicker Man! It's a voodoo doll!"

Willy strolled around the corner and grabbed her in his arms. Stroking her hair as she sobbed and calming her like one of her agitated hens.

"Shhh babes, what has upset you. Sweet heart calm down." He wiped her tears from her face.

The strong warm arms and the caring hands and voice, so calming in comparison to Gervais' recent disinterest, made Tamsin buckle and she stretched forward and kissed Willy with a ferocity she did not know she could possess. Before long the barn was open and the kissing was returned with ragged breaths and clutching at each other's skin.

15 minutes later the dishevelled pair looked at each other coyly. "Don't worry" said Willy, "Good as it was, it stays between you, me and the barn door. What on earth upset you so much?"

Tamsin pointed a shaking finger at the little figure made from straw. It smiled a felt pen face back at her.

Tamsin later looked at the corn dolly and wondered if the curse had made this happen. Did it have any pins in it? Was it her or Gervais or perhaps Willy? Her body ached for Willy's arms. A thrill arced through her insides as she remembered the size of his chest and her hands wrapped over his muscles whilst her legs became entwined with his.

Willy luckily was as good as his word, feeling a little guilty for his unintended marriage wrecking, but rather chuffed at having "had relations" with a famous model, he was determined to find out who had left the doll and never mentioned their dalliance to anyone. Most unlike Willy to be discrete!.

Digging had started and Gervais had become excited. This was the first time that he had tried anything as big as this. He stood on the land and watched as the first cut was made. He had hoped Tamsin would be interested, but she seemed so caught up in her own business - that and Willy. He looked down at his tightening belly and tested his muscles. Not bad he mused, but he was no Willy. Still he had more money and more brains. Or at least worldliness, he mused.

The digger worked throughout the drizzly morning, its noise disturbing the birds and knocking the yellowing leaves. It dug deeper and deeper until it had reached through the fertile top soil and past the heavier clay.

There were so few stones, marvelled Gervais, it would be perfect for straight root vegetables. Stones in the ground would cause the vegetables to grow around them or branch into two, creating legs and willies. He remembered them from the old days when he would snigger at the green grocers.

He must tell Tamsin at some point, they would be great to sell next year. Some of the supermarkets were beginning to sell wonky veg due to a successful local campaign by a TV star that had moved from London to be filmed making his living in the country, just a few miles further towards the coast. He didn't want to miss the boat this time.

Tamsin was busy creating handmade decorations from holly, fir cones and lots of white spray. Her eyes were drifting onto Willy's muscles whilst he sawed through the pallets and made them into recycled crates.

Six fifty-nine flashed red on the led alarm in the dark of Tamsin and Gervais's alarm clock. It was still dark. Gervais shot into the air, his heart racing and he grabbed his phone. "Shit who is it?"

"Sorry mate I can't make it in today, feel bloody awful, like I've been on the sauce all night. Bloody aching and sick. My chest is killing me. Can you go and cover the hole with a tarpaulin so it doesn't fill up with rain? Hold it down with the loose stones and put a few lights or reflector from the van on it.

I hope to be back tomorrow."

Gervais grunted. Early mornings were not his thing, though he did realise that it was not that early a morning.

He mentally calculated his adjustment to the day. Check the sheep, feed the ducks and then go and buy the tarpaulin before the rain due tonight. Use some of the stone left over from the restoration work to secure it.

He yawned as he flopped down the stairs and put the kettle on. He pushed the white spray foliage off the table and yelped as he made contact with the sharp holly leaves. The drizzle was returning so he mentally changed the order of his day to ensure the tarpaulin was a priority.

Whilst sipping his hot coffee and sinking his teeth into sharp marmalade on home baked craft bread, he decided that he wanted to go and have a good look at his hole and compare the land to the plans that his architect had drawn up. Gervais was not concerned about planning permission, not realising it could take years and lots of money to get it granted. He was not aware that if retrospective permission was not granted, he would have to pull down the lot.

Later in the day, he lay on the floor with his head down onto the hole, stroking the earth. He then jumped into the huge depths and shouted "It's all mine!" He never believed he could be a land owner. Now he was becoming a property investor. He hauled over the tarpaulin and placed a few stones on it to hold it in place. It was not windy and Gary would be back on the site tomorrow to look at the earth. It didn't need to be heavily secured. He borrowed a traffic cone from the collection dumped off the back of Gary's van and shoved it close. It was off the road, in his field. That would do.

That evening Tamsin and he sat in front of the TV. Whilst Coronation Street entertained the room, Tamsin googled Christmas decorations and Gervais read the new local paper.

Hmmm there was a 2-page article on the new areas designated for housing development. The local Government were trying to provide affordable homes for the locals since the original properties were being forced to such high prices by people relocating after selling their council flats for half a million in London.

There seemed to be uproar. Arguments from both political camps, residents whose properties would halve in value as their land was encroached by affordable flats and small estates, discussion about which areas of beauty should be sacrosanct. Discussion about turning over old planning restrictions. He looked closer at the map and saw that Norton Beauchamp was on the map. He looked closer and his heart jumped into his throat as he saw a red cross over his land.

"Ancient covenant" it read. "Based on a curse. Nerves of steel required."

Gervais gulped. He began to scratch his arm and noticed a red itchy sore. He scratched again and the sore began to throb.

Gary was not in the following day. The day after, he was in hospital, vomiting blood.

Gervais began to see more red itches on his arm, with black centres forming. No-one went near the tarpaulin and it lay poorly secured, flapping in the rain and wind.

Chapter 17

Halloween resulted in another good night at the pub, but this time for the younger families. By half past six many mini ghosts and witches were traipsing around the village carrying lanterns made from traditional beets and mangle wurzels. These original lanterns produce a more human face, pale and gnarled with hairs on the chin.

Tradition dictates that those home owners with a pumpkin outside the door, are joining in the game and those without do not get bothered.

It was in South Somerset that the tradition of punkie night had begun. Walking back from the barn dance in Chiselborough to Hinton St George on All Hallows Eve, the ladies got fed up waiting for the return of the men. So up for a laugh, they carved faces in the freshly dug beets and lay in wait to terrify their men folk.

The younger generation would dress in the local supermarket produced costumes and move around the village, knocking on the doors of those lit up with pumpkins. Some were locally grown, but many were bought from Asda for £2. Most of the time it was a good chance for the parents to have a catch-up chat with their neighbours since the mud and rain had become a natural curfew. Some villagers would take it upon themselves to terrify the trick or treaters with impressive displays and scary noises as they opened their doors.

After the "trick or treating" had been completed, it was only right that the parents got some time in the pub whilst the little monsters ran around terrifying each other.

John smiled at the squeals of the gathering children and passed over glasses of wine and lager to the happy parents and sweets to the trick or treaters.

No tricks were ever played of course because everyone was joining in. It was a proper country fun family evening although it was often the young ghouls that walked their parents' home by the end of it all.

Shortly afterwards came the next autumn celebration.

Bonfire night was organised by the parish council committee.

Everyone gathered in the village hall, sipping mulled wine and sharing anecdotes about their gardens and the Halloween pub night. The mothers chatted together whilst the children ran in a circuit up and down the stairs and across the stage.

Sparklers were traded and the countdown begun. Sarah reminded everyone, including her own children, to wipe the sparklers in the wet grass to cool them and then put all the rubbish in the bin liners tied to stakes so the cows would not eat it.

The doors were opened and everyone ran to the field to get a glimpse of Guy Fawkes being torched. Huge cheers arose as he ignited despite the wet autumn.

Soon the volley of fireworks begun. Babies were held close and older children screamed and cheered as the rockets forged into the air to break with an ear-splitting noise, into gentle flowers.

Tamsin breathed in the clear air and revelled in the shared cheer. So nice to be part of a village where you knew everyone and not just a face in a crowd. She slipped her arm in Gervais's and returned his smile.

In London, Diwali and sometimes Eid occurred at a similar time to bonfire night. Fireworks pounded the streets from late September through to the end of November. Some youths had begun to use them horizontally as weapons and the fun had been replaced by fear.

The sky was still cloudy and damp. The heavy grey reflected the colours of the fireworks into an eerie orange and red blur and forced the embers close to the viewers. It felt like the blitz to the older residents.

"Oi watch my thatch Phelps!" The heckle came from the crowd and everyone roared with laughter.

Jane smiled at Phelps.

"Well done partner, we did the village proud again!"

Phelps flicked off the slug that had travelled through the long grass and adhered to his steel toe-capped boot.

"Super job partner! Fancy a hog roast bun?"

Helen sat in the pub with John. She felt the family event too painful to attend. It used to be her parents that organised bonfire night. The Phelps took it over with her good wishes to keep it going, but she had not been able to support it herself.

When Jane and Phelps came in with the throng of firework revellers, she slipped away.

The post bonfire party had not been organised. John had attempted discussion with Clara but gave in after bruised ribs.

Everyone flooded back to the pub anyway. The children were allowed in for a few hours, until it became too raucous. It was the parents second chance of the season to meet and let their hair down, until they became a little wobbly.

The children would sit in a group, sharing gaming tips on their parent's phones. The younger ones would play with pocket ponies and soft toys until they slumped under coats or begged their parents to leave.

Shane was getting amorous as the beer flowed. He wandered around slapping the younger single mother's rumps and tried to get in on their conversation. He was tolerated with humorous retorts and returned slaps.

Clara stood on the steps and smiled. She was right, a good pub didn't need gimmicks. She went to bed and slept peacefully.

Later, so did John.

The following evening, John was stiff. The bonfire night had exhausted him. Being the only one behind the bar was too much.

He was fed up with having to fight to get the pub to a functioning level. Helen was not in quite so regularly and he was missing her bright smile. He was also worried by Pam, who was getting weak in her hind quarters and becoming more regularly incontinent.

John decided to pour himself a stiff drink to release his own stiffness. Time to broach it again.

He was going to do something about it finally. He didn't know what, but something had to change.

Clara was sitting on the sofa watching a program following the construction of high end architect designed houses when John finished and went upstairs. She raised a red wine stained glass and mumbled. He topped it up for her.

Clara, I am going to ask Helen to come in a work in the bar a couple of times a week. Speed up the service so we can sell more.

We need to clean the place up and make it more of a family pub. You saw the success we had last night, we can do more of that, but I need help.

"What are you not capable of running a pub? Who needs gimmicks to get people in the door? What is wrong with you? You just want that girl down there so you can stare at her, you lecherous, incompetent hopeless fool!"

"For God's sake Clara, can't you see sense? I ...*we* need help down there, the place is going to rack and ruin, all the trade is going to the Prince of Wales. Would you drink in that tip down there and look at my miserable face?"

She's not going to muscle in on my pub and my husband! Dirty tramp. Bet she has been putting these thoughts in your head. She will be plotting my demise and getting into my shoes as soon as she can!

I'm going over to see that tart now! Tell 'er to keep away dirty slag. You aint going to spend our income on 'aving 'er around to lust after."

She leapt up and grabbed a bottle and swung it down on the table.

John knew what would happen next. A surge of anger washed through him. He was not going to get hit again. With a roar, he leaped towards her to grab the bottle. Both crashed to the floor.

The sores on Gervais' arms were spreading and he was feeling distinctly ill. Flu like symptoms, heaviness and itching. The project was put on hold. Gary was in isolation. Nobody seemed to know what to do. As he lay in bed, Gervais began to think about the curse. What was it the newspaper said?

"You stupid stupid fool!" He moaned. "That bloody covenant was there for a reason!"

Chapter 18

"Thank you for coming together again so soon. I wanted to know how we are all getting on with the *Secret Campaign*."

There was a loud slam and a scraping of claws and Helen rushed in, cheeks glowing. "Sorry everyone."

Everyone grunted, smiled or raised their pints. Phelps raised his eyes and met hers. Helen gave a flash of a conciliatory smile. Both swept their eyes away quickly. Inside Helen's heart began to race and he hands shook as she took a long gulp on her pint.

"Willy, I hear that you have had rather an effect on Tamsin." Jane looked at Willy who dropped his eyes and a slight glow reached his cheeks.

"How did the pallet hiding go?"

"Oh yes! Willy realised the form of effect that Jane was alluding to. "I have managed a few spookers and reminded her over and over about the curse. She said that she is going to look it up at Taunton Museum. Trouble is, she is so obsessed with that bloody shop that she isn't really bothered about the curse."

"Did you see my newspaper report? About village development?"

"Ha ha" guffawed Shane *"Nerves of steel required"*. Liked that bit"

"By the way, who was it who left the corn dolly. Tamsin was telling me about it in the shop. Gave her a real scare apparently. You Ok Willy, you look a bit hot, was that you?"

"No, I think it might have been Jake." Said Helen. "I was learning about patrons with Jake and he made me a corn doll. He said he was going to put one out for Tamsin to find."

"OOOHHHH Jakey boy, who is heeeee" Chorused Shane.

A flash of irritation crossed Phelps's face and was quickly controlled.

"Um." Said Helen "He is a gypsy who is squatting on the bottom of Romany Bubble. I met him walking the dogs and we have been talking about horse whispering and the like."

"Hold on hold on!" Burst in Jane. "Did you say they are squatting on the land Gervais is trying to develop? Has he seen them yet? Do you realise what this means? How long have they been there?"

"Steady Jane." Murmured Phelps and put his hand out as a warning.

"Oh God, Have I done wrong, Oh God" Helen paled and her knees buckled. She sat heavily and drained her pint. "Please tell me I haven't done anything wrong again."

Phelps held her hand and looked closely in her eyes.

"Helen, you have never done anything wrong. Please believe me."

He clutched her hand and Helen began to realise things were going to be all right between them again.

"Jane means that this could have pretty much solved the problem."

Again, Helen wasn't sure which problem, if not both, had been solved.

"Squatters laws right!" said Shane "Gonna cost a whole wad of money and take a whole load of time to get rid of them. I know! Done it meself!"

Everyone cheered and raised their pints.

"By the way, are you alright, John? You have been rather quiet today."

"Well I dunno whatta do really, Clara seems to have left me. I got up this morning after another row and 'er as disappeared. Left 'er this morning to cool down, but I thought 'er would be back by tonight. Been five hours without booze, she gotta be in trouble."

"Hmm do you want to set up a search? Have you called the police?" Phelps took over with instinctive military precision.

"No, they won't do anything for over 24 hours. She is supposed to be a grown up remember."

"Would they consider her a vulnerable adult?"

"The only thing vulnerable about her is me."

A few mutters were heard.

"Right let's go through the details then and work out what to do." Phelps began to rally up the troops.

"Well I dunno really, 'er was about to 'it me with a bottle and I went to grab it and I dunno what happened. I woke up this morning with a banging headache and a few bruises and no wife."

"Christ!" said Shane "You poor bugger, I knew she was a bit of a tyrant, but what has she been up to?"

To everyone's amazement John collapsed into tears. He pulled up the front of his greying shirt to reveal layers of bruising at different stages of black, purple and yellow.

"Has Clara been doing this to you?" Jane gasped. John nodded. "She's been at it for years."

There was a collective gasp and similar gestures of worry. John was asked for more details and everyone sat back stunned as John released his restraint on the story.

Phelps was quick to divvy everyone up into a search party. "Jane, can you stay here with John?"

"It is pitch black and raining out there. Wait until tomorrow."

"Ok first light tomorrow, that's about 7:30. Let's start looking in the area".

"Helen, you 'aint 'erd anything?"

"Me why?"

"'Er was cross with you cos I wanted to ask you to help in the pub. Thought you and I were 'aving an affair."

Most people laughed but Phelps and Helen both felt a nauseating surge rise in their stomachs.

Helen was finding herself the centre of too much tonight and for the following week she made herself ill repeating the events and possible scenarios' over and over in her head. Her stomach continually clenched and pumped acid into her mouth. Her heart pounded and she felt weak with the ugly thoughts crowding her head. She continually rethought the situation, considering what she did wrong and rerunning the scenario, correcting it all in her mind.

Most of all she felt guilty about the little jokes that she had shared with

John about how to "Finish Clara off". Inventive as they were and as far as she was concerned a comical way to finish a pint, perhaps John had gone ahead with one of those plans. Would she Helen be an instigator? Had she been part of something terrible that she didn't even want to admit to herself.

By the end of that weekend, before she was aware of the events around her, Helen's house was shining and freshly painted, her hands raw and her eyes red from the pounding cortisol that took over her entire being. Betsy had no signs of being Nutter anymore because Helen had been exercising her very thoroughly each morning before normal people arose.

As her brain finally began to regain control of her body, she began to find herself forgetful and clumsy and she hated herself more and more.

Keeping herself locked away however, protected her from the events that were unfolding in the village.

That night, the rain had stopped and the full moon hung low in the sky like a yellow lantern. The wet hardened to a sharp frost, covering the already wet branches with a hard-shiny white resin. The grass became like fragile shards of grass, ready to snap underfoot. The mud turned into rock solid mountains and valleys where it had been turned over by footsteps and tractor tyres. Clouds of snowy white breath puffed like icing sugar from the animal's nostrils as the competed with each other for the morning's delivery of hay and warmed beet. Car owners turned on their engines and heaters before they settled to their breakfast, sending syrupy pollution clouds into the air.

At first light, which was now 7.30 am since the clocks had gone back, the villagers gathered in front of the pub with walking sticks and cameras in case they needed to record any information. They had decided not to call the police yet, but to find her themselves and support John how they could. Phelps was feeling guilty because he had not noticed what poor John had been going through. He had been wrapped up so much in his own problems – all his own making, that he hadn't considered that anyone else might be in trouble.

"Right" began Phelps, "shall we split up and do a general search first and then get more detailed if necessary. She can't drive and none of us drove her anywhere. She hasn't booked a taxi, John checked, so she must be out here somewhere. Let's hope she is just sleeping off that booze and isn't too hurt. Shane and Willy, will you take the river side, God hope she didn't fall in there. It is still full of summer weed that could pull her down.

Jane and I will do our gamekeeper land and out to Romany Bubble. Give us a chance to chat to those gypsies down there about their plans. Helen said she is not well enough to join us at the moment.

Tom and Estella, can you go over the farm fields at the back of the pub? Jim and Sarah, can you do the barns on the farms. Don't forget to go as far as Gervais's because they have been doing some nice work over there with Willy, she may have sheltered in one of them."

"Aye Aye Captain!" Shouted Shane. Phelps flushed and muttered an apology.

"No, Phelps! Ye be good in your praaaper position, sortin' us all out prapper job. Bedder than thee being Captain Mannerin' coun'ry gent all the time!"

Phelps blushed again but quietly dropped the affectation from his language.

"Here is the list of everyone's mobile numbers so we can get together once we find something."

Everyone nodded their consent and set off on the first beautiful morning of winter. The bright sun was warming the thatches, causing the rooftops to steam into the blue sky. The trees were already dripping and the mud returning to its usual consistency. Everybody had heavy boots and waxed jackets or high visibility waterproofs. Shane had his usual well worn fatigues on. The beaters had brought their black labs and spaniels to help with the smelling out, they were highly trained to disturb the pheasant and hopefully would help sniff out Clara.

Jane and Phelps strode over the land that they managed. They walked close to the hedges occasionally disturbing pheasants that would raise vertically out of the long grass with squawking heavy flaps. Their black lab Aga was running in zig zags across the cobweb jewelled ground with his nose down and his tail up.

"What do you think has happened? You see more of John and Clara than I do." Jane asked.

"Hmm she has been a bit of a nightmare recently, but I didn't realise that she was regularly beating him. He kept that covered up well. She has been drinking more recently and she is looking totally shot away most of the time. Wonder is Helen is ok? Do you think we should drop by? I think she felt she had a bit of a beating at that meeting."

"No leave her be, she doesn't need to know about this, we can swing back up onto the road as we hit the plantation and the valley."

"I love mornings like this, all orange, autumnal and crisp. Shame we are out for such a morbid reason."

"I love you Jane." Said Phelps suddenly and he meant it more than ever. She was such a rock, she had put up with so much from him, with the nightmares and the moods. Heaven knows she married a naval officer, not a game keeper and their income was nowhere near what it was.

Jane smiled and squeezed his hand.

Shane and Willy knew they had been given the tough job. They would have the strength to pull her out of the river and hopefully the guts to handle what they faced. They progressed slowly along the bank, looking carefully, poking the reeds and the rotting invasive Himalayan Balsam with their sticks in case they disturbed something.

"Bloody rape, gets everywhere." Grumbled Willy as he tripped through the pods of seeds that cross pollinated from the fields. Bright yellow and beautiful along the river banks in May, now they were just a trip hazard.

As they wandered, a strange almost croaking sound grew louder from behind them. They both looked up as an arrow shape of swans flew above them. It wasn't a rare sight as the swans spent much of their time on the rhynes of the levels. But it was always a treat to watch as they stretched out their long white necks and powered through the sky the blue of the sky tinting their wings.

"Tis amazing that they can go so fast, huge things that they are."

"They are so regal and graceful, bet you wouldn't catch one of them behaving badly. Puts us humans to shame."

Both men drew the comparison of the pure white beauty of the swans to the gnarled, alcohol destroyed face of Clara and walked in silence for a while.

Tom and Estella were working hard as they squelched through melting mud. The earth that had only recently been dry, sandy cracked paths, between the tall crops, was now just part of the shaven slop with occasional heads of stubble. Their feet were sinking heavily and so they were having to half jog with bent knees to try not to sink too deeply.

"She can't be out here. Really?" said Estella. If she was as drunk as she usually is, she wouldn't have been able to progress over this. We should have a re-think.

"Let's get to the end of this field and get onto the grass. I think you are right. Where else could she have gone? If she was cross with Helen, surely she would have gone to sort her out?

You don't think Helen has bashed her over the head and buried her, do you?"

"Is that why she hasn't come out on the search? She looked alright last night at the meeting. Mind she has been a bit weird recently"

Both laughed but then realised that they may be rather close to the truth and began to trudge on towards Helen's house with a queasy feeling in their stomachs.

Jim and Sarah had been wandering inside the barns. Many were filled with young steers that were to be brought on over the winter and sold as meat in spring. The sweet smell of hay combined with the breath of the cows and the wet noses snuffling was a true delight.

"Think that we got the good job aye Jim?"

"Arrr. There's nothing like the smell of young stock in barns."

"Let's hope there isn't a drunk woman in a barn. Surely she would have woken by now? She must be injured or something. God I hope she didn't fall asleep outside, it could be the end of her with that sharp frost."

"Unless she has got herself locked in somewhere. Perhaps we should knock on the doors and get them to look."

"You don't think John is covering up, do you? I wouldn't imagine that he would be so upset. She is such a cow, but do you think that he finally hit her back? Is she in the freezer or under the skittle alley? Was it guilt that made him break down like that last night?"

"Step carefully young Sarah, don't 'ee say a word. Whether 'ee be right or wrong, we don't want our John put away. She deserves what 'er de get if ye ask me."

"You're right. Mum's the word."

They headed towards Manor Farm and looked forward to seeing some more of Tamsin's creations. The shop was beginning to bring in a lot of trade. Lots of women wanting to see a model in real life, and men were buying gifts for their wives so they could grab a gander at the fit bird in the village.

The barn had certainly been tidied up. Willy had been working hard. Outside rested a collection of old machinery, milk churns and tractor seats that had been pulled out of the barn and the undergrowth. Seeing a flash of movement through the window, Sarah and Jim decided to knock before they went to the barns.

Tamsin answered the door in a dressing gown with tangled hair and mascara smudged eyes. She paled as the two visitors recounted the tale. Grabbing her yard boots and new Barbour, she came out into the yard and opened the barn.

Instead of the scent of straw, there was a smell of warm cinnamon.

"Sorry for the smell, I am making Christmas spice wraps for mulled wine."

Both Sarah and Jim drew in the heady sweet smell with pleasure.

"You are more than welcome to look around the land. I can come with you but I am not sure that she would have reached this far would she? I mean why on earth would she walk out in the dark anyway?"

The pair explained the connection with Helen and that they were considering if she had drunkenly walked across the yard to short cut across Romany Bubble to Helen's house.

"Well we can walk a little way across The Bubble if you like, see if she has tripped over in the hedge or something. Hell, you don't think she has made it to Gervais's hole?"

Everybody began to run, feet clumping heavily in thick mud resistant boots, slipping on the wet grass and churned up gateways.

And there at the bottom of the eight-foot drop, enshrouded in muddy yellow tarpaulin, was a small and crumpled body dressed in red.

Chapter 19

"Think!" groaned Phelps.

"Before we go down and get her, should we touch the scene? Is she alive?"

Everyone peered cautiously into the hole and muttered.

"Let's call 999 and get some advice."

"Ah but us need to get our stories straight, we dun want our Jarn to get int trouble do us?" Jim cut in.

"No, quick, get John over here, Jane can you phone everyone to get over here now. Sarah, can you call 999. We need to see John's first reaction, give him time to compose himself before the police get here. Not that I think he did anything, but God let's try some damage limitation."

"What 'bout our 'Elen, tis 'er we need to tell, cos Clara was after her won 'er?" Shane interjected.

"No leave poor Helen for the moment, she looked like she was about to go under again last night. This would really finish her off. Spare her some recovery time."

"Right you are."

Before long, the rest of the search party arrived. They were followed shortly by the ambulance and police. The party had been warned not to touch and that the ambulance would get there quickly. There was one resting in Ilminster and one in Martock and they would be here rapidly. They knew the area so well after the myriad of call outs to accidents on the A303 that it would not take long. The damage of a night in the frost had already been done.

John looked on white faced. He seemed to be in a state of shock. He said nothing but began to violently shake. Tamsin collected him a blanket from her Christmas collection and place it over his shoulders.

Gervais meanwhile had been in bed, still poorly. He ached and was nauseous and the sores were beginning to itch on his arms. He was the type of man who feared the doctors and would happily put it off over and over.

The sirens startled him into action and he hauled himself over to the window.

"Shit shit Christ! What has happened? Tamsin!"

Gervais pulled on his dressing gown and socks, grabbed his boots and was out of the door as the bed was pulled out of the ambulance.

Sadly, the effort was too great for his poorly body and as he reached his trench, his knees buckled and his stomach convulsed sending blood and vomit over the ground.

Tamsin screamed. Christ, she hadn't realised that he was so poorly. Red hot waves of guilt began to form over her body as she realised what she had been up to whilst her husband was getting ill.

The paramedics rushed into action whilst the police called for an emergency response vehicle.

John, Clara and Gervais were swept into Musgrove Hospital whilst the search party looked on helplessly.

Chapter 20

Tamsin was sitting in the kitchen. She had been told to go home and wait. Gervais was alive, Clara was not and now the medical professionals needed to stabilize, diagnose and autopsy.

The noise from the scullery was smashing into her thoughts. Tamsin went to look at her spring and saw that it was belting out into the Belfast sink.

"You can sense trouble, can't you. It's almost like you are the voice of Tom, trying to tell me something."

The spring churned and slapped in response.

Right, to Taunton Museum you reckon. I will go and find out about this blessed curse and then go and see if they have found out what is wrong with Gervais.

The spring seemed to quieten. Tamsin smiled to herself. Bloody curses and talking springs. What was happening to her sense of reality since she moved to the country?

Tamsin admired the huge ivy covered castle gates and the ancient buildings clustered around a courtyard in the centre of Taunton. She slipped through the huge glazed doors of the museum and went to ask for some help.

The historians were delighted to help and they set about finding information on the curse.

"There were many settlements that do not exist now because of the drainage and reclamation of the moors and levels. Perhaps there was one on your land. Let's look through the old maps and find out."

Several hours later and Tamsin was thanking her lucky stars it was Sunday free parking, a map was found of Romany Bubble and sure enough, there was an ancient village there.

"Looks like there was a settlement called *"Combe Burble"*. The Combes are the steep sided valleys that were formed by the ancient rivers. Think Odcombe, Templecombe, Combe St Nicholas, Monkton Combe. Look your area is just south of the moors and in the Hamstone region. Ham Hill was an ancient settlement that looked over the flooded moors that gave Somerset its name. Many of the villages were submerged in the winter and only emerge in summer. Ham means hill as does burrow, lots of villages have these names here. Super defences, you can see for miles across the kingdom. Next stop like this was Cadbury Castle nearly 15 miles across the low-lying moors to the East."

It says that word of mouth history suggests that the village was torched in the 1800's and a covenant put on it, not to break the surface of the land.

Hmm I wonder why they left. Was it witch craft?

Oh look! Anthrax!"

Tamsin recoiled in horror. Wasn't that the name of a heavy metal band? It must be something hideous then. Wasn't it something they did to the Vietnamese in the war?

"Anthrax is a bacterial illness that can be contracted by cows and humans. It can take on several forms depending on how it is contracted. Flu like symptoms, sores on the arms. Vomiting blood.

There are registered outbreaks of anthrax in the area in the past, the latest ones being in the 1980's and just recently in 2015. All cows and barns are burned to prevent it spreading, but it is possible for spores to lie dormant in the ground until disturbed.

Your ancient village was torched to the ground according to this. Seems like the local witchcraft group were brought in to clear a curse. They chanted and made spells to clear the earth of the curse before completely eradicating the village. The surviving members went to seek their fortunes in Yeovil, Stoke Sub Hamdon and Martock in the gloving industry that was developing in the 1800's. A covenant was put on the land to prevent the curse arising again.

I see it was renamed Romany Bubble as the unusable land was let out to the gypsies to stay on whilst harvesting time. In particular, the special

Martock bean that is grown in the area. Oh yes! Look, the bubble bit is that spring and little river through the middle. Hang on, not one spring, but three, one seems to be right in the hillside by the farm there."

"Not by the farm! In the farm!" exclaimed Tamsin. "It's my bit of the bubble, it flows right into the scullery!"

The museum curator smiled, infected by her enthusiasm.

"Now what are the symptoms of Anthrax? Here you go. It depends on how it is contracted. You can inhale it, get it in the skin from working with animal skins and eat it. Seems like chills, sores and at its worst v and d with blood."

Tamsin paled and then flushed as the sense of guilt hit her. She had been planning to research this for ages and instead she got caught up in her own little world making pretty things and having sex with a lad 10 years younger than her. She should have seen that Gervais was ill and been caring for him. Instead she had been unfaithful to him, not only with another man, but with her thoughts. He may be skinny and not so attractive, but she married him. She married him for security and to make sure she didn't end up poor and bitter like her mother. She married him because she knew that men were users and so why shouldn't she do the same? Love may not have come into it but he was a good man and she had abused that.

Then within a flash she began to feel angry. Greedy man with his middle-class ways, thought he could ride rough shod over people's knowledge and wishes because he wanted to make more money. If he hadn't been so greedy and desperate to get started, the planning people would have looked into the covenant and the history of the area before giving permission. He would not be in the situation he was if he hadn't rushed to get started.

Her stomach dropped and then flew into her mouth. Gervais and she could be up for manslaughter. Silly Clara fell into a hole on our ground, insufficiently protected and probably raging with anthrax spores. Oh God and there was Gary the ground worker. They hadn't even bothered to visit him.

Tamsin sat down heavily and watched her carefully constructed world begin to unravel.

Chapter 21

The police were getting busy. John had been questioned twice. Once in hospital as he was treated for shock and then at the police station.

Inspector Jack was deep on thought and drawing questions together.

There was nothing wrong with the publican's story, but it was full of holes, well one big gaping hole. He didn't know what happened to him that evening. He couldn't account for his whereabouts apart from that he thought he was passed out after an attack from his wife.

Could he have pushed her in the trench out of spite, or did he hit her and then drag her into the trench?

What the hell was she doing out in the fields anyway? She didn't look like the sort to go for walks in the country in a little red dress.

Hurry up post mortem!

John had been ordered in to have a full medical to prove that Clara had been beating him.

Poor John didn't think it was possible to be more humiliated unless he was having a full drug trafficking search. The police medical staff stripped him and poked him, checking all his bruising and trying to date the injuries.

It looked like he was telling the truth.

Helen was due a visit too. Did Clara make it to her house? Did they have a scuffle and did Helen push her into the trench. Did she strangle or hit her over the head and then drag her into it? Perhaps Helen had heard the weather forecast and knew a blind drunk 50 something would not survive the night?

What about the land owners? Were they part of it? They must be liable for leaving a barely covered unlit trench on their property. Were they involved or just plain daft?

Inspector Jack decided it was high time to visit the Helen and then the ex-model and her popstar husband. If nothing else, it would be a pleasant afternoon being looked after by the beautiful Tamsin.

Jane and Phelps were lying low. They had nothing to prove or to say. The search party had agreed on their story and were backing John with reports of the frequent injuries and how he had become subdued. The ones who could give him an alibi for the pub the previous evening were prompted to report to the police to do so. Everyone silently prayed that this horrible event would pass.

Only Jane felt a tinge of sadness for the loss of a life.

Phelps was beginning to feel the guilt rise in him again. It nagged and chewed away at every thought, leaving him sick, pale and listless.

If he hadn't kissed Helen, she would never have sought refuge in the pub. Clara would not have become jealous and then none of this would have happened.

"Silly selfish prick!" He screamed inside. What had he done to his wife, his almost daughter and his good mate in the pub?

Shane told the police that Clara had been dead inside for years and that she was a rude hysterical drunkard that had been no use to anyone. He vouched that John was far too gentle to have done anything like that.

The police saw a simple chap living in run down rented accommodation with wood chip wall paper and ripped tarpaulins covering oily vehicle parts in the drive. A character somewhat anachronistic, never having progressed from the 90's traveller culture that dominated Somerset a few decades ago and could be widely revisited on a trip to Glastonbury. Would he be credible in court?

Luckily Helen had not yet been questioned because of course she knew that John had considered alcohol poisoning for his wife's demise and they had giggled over it at the bar.

Willy reported that the trench had been covered by tarpaulins hastily after the ground worker had been rushed to hospital. Since then the land owner had also been ill and so it hadn't come to anyone's attention that the trench was dangerous. It was on private property after all and everybody knew about it as it was the talk of the village.

Jane as head of the village committee was asked to describe John. She had reported a gentle, if not exhausted man who battled to be a lovely host even when his wife shouted obscenities at him in public. She wondered aloud to the police, if they should have noticed more and what they should have done.

"Hurry up post mortem", sighed Jack again.

First thing on the Tuesday morning, the post mortem result was in. Jack could reveal that Clara had not been beaten what so ever. She had died of exposure to the sub-zero, wet evening. She had bruises consistent with the fall and had been timed to have died during that night.

Her body had then been frozen in the harsh frost of the following evening.

Would she have been saved if they had searched for her on the morning that she went missing? Unlikely, she was already dead from a skin-full of alcohol a shock to the system, internal bleeding and exposure the same night she had marched from her home.

Her tiny bird like hands were also pitted with bruising and John's bruises were consistent with the size of her tiny knuckles.

"So just Helen to fit in to all this." Sighed Jack. "How the hell did Clara end up getting into the trench? Did she have some help? Forensics said they couldn't find any other finger prints and the edge of the trench was mired up by the search party.

Chapter 22

Inspector Jack paid a visit to Helen.

He found a shrunken drawn woman in an excessively clean house. Was she guilty? She damn well looked it. She spoke fast, without a break and then would stare off into the distance. He wasn't sure it he had heard her talking to her mother earlier but he had checked and knew both parents were deceased.

She had told a story of a frightening women who had ruled the pub with an iron fist, hurling obscenities at the locals and refusing to update the pub.

"Why do you think Clara was over near your house in the dark?"

"My house! Is that what you think? Are you sure she was not over with Gervais and Tamsin?"

"According to John, she was angry with you and was going to give you a piece of her mind."

Helen quaked and looked smaller than ever. Inspector Jack wondered if this was her usual stance or was it the recollection of events that affected her. How could something as small and terrified as this, create such a reaction in a woman who beat her husband?

"What do you think made Clara so angry?"

"I pop into the pub on my dog walks. Living alone, it is a good way to be sociable. I think she thought I was after John. We chatted lots at the bar, when we were the only ones in there."

"Did she love him?"

"I suppose so, in her way. She was just such an angry woman though. She hated people using the pub as a social venue. She wanted it to be a hard-drinking establishment, not a community meeting place.

I think she was worried that I was changing things perhaps. We did get excited about renovation plans together."

"Why were you not on the hunt for her the next day?"

"I.. I didn't know about it. Perhaps they thought I would be too useless."

"Useless?"

"Well I am not good at much, riding horses yes, but I failed in my teaching career and I don't seem to be doing very well at relationships...." She faltered feeling her throat begin to constrict.

"Can you prove where you were on that night?"

"Um, I was in the pub at about 4 o'clock, after walking Pootle. I dropped in on a friend before that."

Helen clasped her hand to her mouth. Shit! She mustn't reveal where Jake was or he would get evicted.

"What about after that?"

"Uh uh I was at home. I was on the internet, I guess you could look at the time of my emails and down loads, would that let you know I was at home?"

"Certainly, if I take your iPad, I can probably have it back for you in a couple of days, unless there is evidence on it."

"Sure, I have my iPhone."

"Better take that too!"

Inspector Jack left and Helen slumped in her seat.

About an hour afterwards she had a knock on the door. Her heart leapt into her throat. She forced it down with a swallow and pulled herself up to answer it, pushing back a delighted looking Pootle who was dancing circles around her feet.

"Jake!" Helen's spirits rose and the grey from her pallor rose to a flush.

"Are you ok? Geez you look terrible! What's been going on? I saw the emergency vehicles and so I be 'idden for a few days, just in case they move us on like. Whaaat? Are you ok?"

The kindness and worry in Jake's dark eyes made Helen crumple and she began to sob, huge chest racking sobs. He wrapped himself around her and held on until the sobbing subsided.

Over a cup of tea, made by Jake, she told him of her situation.

It all came out in mismatched lumps surrounded by sobs. From Clara's death and her possible involvement, to her parents dying and her failing to hold on to her job.

"Hell Helen, I'm not surprised you finally broke down. You've been under so much pressure; you have held on for so long. Eventually something has got to give. You are past the worst now, it is just time to heal."

He held onto her, feeling her fragile warmth against her and he realised that his heart was beginning to belong to her.

Damn he better make sure he didn't make the same mistake as that Phelps chap!

"Would you like me to stay a few days? Just whilst the police are about, moral support like? You have a spare room I can use."

"What about Ellie and the children?"

"Who? Ellie and 'er pestering monsters! No the kids are great, but Dad and Ellie can look after them, they aren't really my responsibility."

Helen stared at him.

"I thought you gypsy families stuck together? Ellie won't let you stay with me, surely?"

"No I love them an' that, but they can do without me a few days, I'm not their Dad after all!"

"But what about Ellie?"

"I may be the man of the group now but Ellie and Eli can manage a few days without me. That cousin of mine is as tough as old boots."

"You and she aren't married, or together?"

"Get stuffed! We gypsies ain't into dodgy stuff like that! She's blood!"

Helen looked up at the sky and mouthed "Thank you!".

Chapter 23

Tamsin had left the museum and had driven as fast as is possible through the congested streets of Taunton, to Musgrove hospital where Gervais and Gary were being monitored.

She had shoved the paperwork in front of the nurses, who had called the Doctors and consultants.

Before long, Gervais and Gary were receiving antibiotics and were gaining strength.

No wonder it was called a curse. Dig the ground and out comes the spores repeatedly decades and centuries after the initial infection.

Tamsin sat with Gervais and watched his recovery.

She began to realise that she was at a turning point in her life. She still had proceeds of her modelling and was realising that she had other skills that she could turn to. Did she need to be married to Gervais anymore? Perhaps it was time to go it alone and just not need to bother with men any more. She had proven to herself that she did have skills that didn't rely on men's need for sex to maintain her financial security.

She looked forward at Gervais and thought back through all the times they had spent and grown together. The engagement ring in her Cristal champagne, the first kiss in a smoky club, their first walk in the park. Her heart softened and she smiled at the memories. Was she ready to lose that?

Perhaps they were ready for a child, to take the next stage in their lives. Now that neither of them thrived on late night partying and she was too old for conventional modelling, now Gervais was not driving all over the country with the band.

She had the choice. Start her business alone, or start her business and a family with Gervais.

Tamsin looked at Gervais and pictured Willy in her mind. What had she been thinking?

She leaned forward and kissed his hand.

"I'm sorry darling, for not giving you all my attention. Let's work together for the next stage in our lives."

John had been looking through the photographs of his time with Clara. He sat and studied the beautiful young women she had been. He had met her when he had been on a course about handling real ale. She was sharing information about how to store London Pride and she had stood, tall and confident at the front of the room.

He had fallen in love with her and taken her out of London, where they bought the country pub together. Perhaps she had not been happy. He had taken her from her own environment and placed it what might as well be a foreign country. Was that why she was always drunk? Was that why she was so angry with him? Did he not listen to what she had wanted?

He began to rifle through her box of belongings. He rifled through old letters and crumpled photographs. He smiled when he found one of the together just when they had bought the pub. There was a large brown envelope with a collection of current invoices. It was for a pub called "The Olive Branch." There was a copy of the deeds. It was in Clara's name.

There was a phone number of a manager. John made up his mind to call.

Later John sat heavily on a chair with his head in his hands. Clara had spent her time upstairs managing the accounts of the string of 3 pubs in London all with the same name. They were hers and now, unless she had made a will that he didn't know about, they were now all his.

"Oh Clara!" he cried. "Eee were so much cleverer than I let 'ee be. I kept 'ee traaapped 'ere be'ind this rotten old pub whilst your 'eart was in a prarper fast movin' business in your place of birth. No wonder you 'it me." "Don't look back in anger" came into his mind. Is that what you were doing when you went after Helen?

Chapter 24

There was something wrong with Pootle. She seemed lethargic, yet when she went to her bed, she spent time cleaning herself and her bed. She seemed to be constantly tugging at her cushion and blankets. She didn't seem so bothered about going out so much. She still seemed to be eating, in fact she seemed to do nothing but eat and clean herself.

Helen phoned up her insurance provider and then took Pootle to the vet. Pootle was exposed to a full medical, the indignity of a thermometer up her bottom and her mouth held open. The conclusion. She was pregnant.

"Poodle mongrels can be worth a lot of money these days. You might be onto something good! Any idea on what they are? "

"Ahem, lurcher?" Helen mused, remembering Pootle's disappearance.

"*Lurcheroodles*, could be an interesting mix. You should get about 4 or 5. We can do an ultra sound to be sure. If she is pregnant, you will need to follow these nutrition guides and add some more protein to her diet. Let her rest. Labradoodles and Cockerpoo's can sell for more than £500 each, so if you follow all the breeding rules, you may be in for making some money!"

Helen left the vets with several leaflets alongside her bill and news to tell Jake.

Inspector Jack decided to close the case. There was not enough evidence to secure a conviction of anyone. Waste of taxpayer's money.

John had obviously been a victim; the scans of his body had been quite frightening. Layer after layer of old bruising. There were no marks on either John or Clara consistent with retaliation.

"Poor Bugger," muttered Inspector Jack. He began to mentally calculate whether he could raise awareness of this under-reported form of domestic violence. Women had shelters to go to. What about the husbands? How sensitive had they been to his needs?

Helen's alibi was secure, she had been using her own internet consistently and variedly throughout the evening. Mindfulness, self-help, and horse whispering seemed to float that young lady's boat.

He had traced her employment to a local struggling primary school and had her identity and sickness confirmed. Perhaps that explained why she looked such a wreck.

Whether action would be taken about the danger of the tarpaulin over the trench was up to John. It was on private land and everyone in the village knew about it. Could be a tough case, was he up to it? Did he want to?

What about Gary, would he press charges against Gervais? He had made a full recovery. Would Gervais be liable for his illness and loss of earnings?

"Death by misadventure". Muttered Jack. "Case closed for Christmas. Let the healing begin."

Chapter 25

The dust began to settle in Norton Beauchamp and working on the next phase of life needed to be started.

Christmas was well on its way. The pub would close for refurbishment and respect for its loss. John was calling for the villager's input into what they would want from their new pub. The money from Clara's life insurance and selling the 3 pubs would keep John and his pub secure for the future.

Gary and Gervais responded to the antibiotics and the anthrax news flew around the world. Every farm was put on high alert and the local cattle were thoroughly tested and given the all clear. Luckily Gervais had not yet started moving and selling his livestock.

Gervais came out of hospital and began to nest with his wife.

Helen and Jake began to discover life together and day by day, Helen lost her grey pallor and began to focus on the here and now. Less time was spent talking to her parents and more to her lover.

Phelps put his energies back into his marriage and his horses. Both were equally surprised and grateful. Jane began to take out the horse Phelps had been given for Helen and they began to realise that riding out together was fun. Grumph, the Shetland was not so sure, but he too was about to find a new lease of life.

Tom and Estella decided to go away to sunnier climes for Christmas. They went on a cruise with the Hendersons.

Shane was wondering how many long winter nights he could enjoy with his lurcher, especially now that the pub was closed. Time to start something wild and adventurous like volunteering or internet dating. Might find himself a good woman in the process.

Gervais was realising that he had a whole plot of land that he could do nothing with. The land was sprayed and the trench finally refilled. He discovered he had a gaggle of squatters who would be difficult to move.

"Do you realise what we have been through in only six months? You could write a book about it!"

Well let's go to the press first shall we? We could sell our story easily now." Tamsin agreed. "Heaven knows you took enough film footage to keep us going for a while. Perhaps if we agree to share proceeds with Gary, he will stay on our side and not press charges.

"Gervais takes on Anthrax!"

"Listen, this land of ours, do you know why it is called Romany Bubble?

The gypsies have settled on the land for years during the harvest season. They took it on after the original village was burned down a few hundred years ago. Well I was thinking that now it is of no building or farm use, what about starting our own gypsy museum? Our own visitor attraction. Perhaps the National Trust could get involved or we could try and get a grant. We can get Willy to help us build an eco-café with a Princes Trust grant and then get Helen and her gypsy lad to demonstrate the history of the gypsies. Their ways are a dying culture. Apparently, they were a huge part of the Somerset countryside. I have been reading about it. Honestly, I have been loving finding out about the history of this place.

This means that the gypsies down there – yes believe it or not they have been there for over 3 months, could stay – as long as they don't invite too many friends and we don't have to pay to evict them.

I can farm the good land and fill the shop to sell as part of the attraction, the active learning museum will be run by Jake and Helen and you can maintain the small holding. Three separate incomes from one set of land. I hear Helen does horse whispering too. Could be a goer for her and make us some rent on the side.

"I think a New Year's party is due. We can tell our resolutions and see what the neighbours think. Get them onside this time! Would it be in bad taste to get them all to dress up as anthrax victims?"

"What about pop stars. Might be safer."

"You really think so?"

Chapter 26

Christmas day arrived.

A crisp blue morning with a thick white frost that sparkled in the bright sun.

As Gervais peered out of the window, a group of three deer stood on the crest of the hill and looked towards him before crashing into the plantation.

He smiled and drew Tamsin towards him. "What a magical place. And it is ours to make even more special." Downstairs their own part of the bubble (still not altered in anyway by Tamsin) tinkled away in agreement.

All the villagers trooped up past the steaming thatches and sparkling diamond panes of the alms houses and under the thick boughs of the dark yew to the church.

Helen glowed as she walked hand in hand with her new beau Jake. She was not yet aware but soon her career would be sorted for her and she would be able to leave her previous existence with peace and a sense of achievement. Ellie, Eli and the children followed behind, waving "Morning" to all in their path and galloping around like their ponies and puppies.

The villagers were aware of the gypsy's role in preventing planning permission and were also aware of the clean living eco settlement they had created. They were "no trouble" to the villagers and so were accommodated.

Phelps and Jane walked hand in hand, taking smiling glances at each other, vibrant in the refreshment of their marriage.

Shane called on John and the two of them wandered up to the church, talking beer and cellar management and the future of the pub. Before long they were slapping each other on the backs and chortling. John had bought himself a pair of red trousers and was trying to persuade Shane to ditch the old army fatigues and join the Country Gent brigade.

Sarah dragged her two children dressed in fairy wings and Christmas jumpers, clutching their new toys and moaning because they wanted to stay at home and eat the festive bounty.

The pews were full as the locals admired the interior of this precious building that they rarely bothered to visit. Many vows were made to make more of their beautiful resource.

The church organ burst into "The Holly and the Ivy." Deep male voices grumbled along with the base notes whereas the ladies sung tunefully. The children slapped the hymn sheets whilst pretending they could read all the difficult words and then practiced getting up and sitting down until a sharp whisper and a grabbed arm prevailed.

"Thank you for coming to join us on this special day." Began the Priest.

"Today I want to think about the concept of forgiveness. We often hear about sad stories when children are killed or maimed. Social Media quickly spreads sad stories about our friends and neighbours far and wide.

We hear the Christian parents say they can forgive their children's attackers and we all wonder how this is possible. Is it the wimp's way out? Forgive so you don't have to stand up for yourself and do something about it?

Well forgiveness is about letting go of the anger and the pain for yourself.

There are many ways of doing this, perhaps with restorative justice, meeting your attacker, understanding why they did it and telling them what it did to you.

When we forgive, we let go of the burden of anger and bitterness and are then able to make happier more satisfying relationships for ourselves. It is not an entirely unselfish act of saying "Hey it doesn't matter mate or being friends with the perpetrator." It is more about coming to terms with your own bitter anger and then letting it go. The perpetrator should still receive the fitting punishment. The punishment is not about lashing back and getting revenge but ensuring that they receive the suitable sanctions and support to make sure they turn their lives around and become a useful part of society.

Remember how Jesus loved everyone, regardless of their background. He loved them and helped them to turn their lives around. Before we judge others by their sins, consider where they have come from and what may make them behave that way. Can we try to forgive their sins so that we can understand and support each other to make the right decisions in the future."

Forgiveness is a Christian teaching that everyone may find useful in managing their own lives."

The congregation muttered their agreements.

"Now to finish off we have some notes for the parish.

Clara's funeral will be held on the 28th of this month followed by a celebration of her life in the pub. John also seeks your ideas on what will make our pub a true village resource so that in her memory, it can be taken to the next stage of its life. He would like you to bring your ideas to her celebration or post and email them."

Gervais and Tamsin also request all villagers to join them for a New Year's party, starting with an announcement for which they would like your input. Sounds intriguing. I can't wait!

Now before we sing our final hymn "Oh Come All Ye Faithful", I would also like to ask you to stay for a few Christmas drinkies in the church before you go and put on the turkey."

The church erupted into a chorus of "Glo…oor…oor..oor ia, Hosannah In excelsis" The children holding their breath until they went purple, giggling as their voices waned to a squeak. Tamsin and Gervais sang confidently whilst Arthur and Jim the older generation kept their deep croaks under their breath. Willy stood by his father nursing a sore head created by an overzealous Christmas catch up with his old mates who had left the area to seek their fortunes in the city. Helen, used to singing at school, enjoyed being able to blast out the words, whilst Jake smiled indulgently at her.

So, for a while the village returned to normal. Buoyed up on the excitement of a new future and a stronger union forged by the distress of the previous months.

Postscript

The summer sun was sending out deep pink daggers into the sky and stretching the shadows as Tamsin and Gervais strolled, arm in arm, through their spotless farm yard. Behind them the blackbird scolded loudly to warn others of their arrival. Both had their free hand resting on the perfectly shaped bump, covered in Boden maternity florals.

They reached out to tickle Grumph's nose as they passed. Helen's horse whispering had made him a gentle delight to the children who visited on their way to the living museum. Close by, a head was snatched up from the grass as Helen's new wild eyed project backed off from their presence.

Jake could be seen tidying the eco house and watering the herb roof before signing off for the evening.

"Thank you, Lottery, for the grant to create this magical place" breathed Tamsin.

The shop had gone from strength to strength now that the living museum was up and running. Willy and Jake had helped create a strong early harvest which was selling well alongside her natural crafts. Jake's gypsy traditions were also selling well, people loved the step back in time to a simpler place.

Customers could choose from a range of activities such as game keeping with Phelps, craft with Tamsin and traditional gypsy life skills with Jake. Helen would take them riding, or walks with the goats. Gervais had continued to develop the remains of the old barn into a self-contained cottage.

They had recently purchased an ancient Romany caravan which Jake and Willy were restoring. Helen was persuading his Gypsy Cobb to respond to the side reins so she could get him in harness. Weekend escapism courses were the next idea. Combining ancient gypsy living with horse therapy and good food. Tamsin was thinking about training as an aromatherapist.

The Lurcheroodles had been a success and Pootle was pregnant with her second batch that were all secured with pre-ordered homes.

Tamsin looked up at the lines of a faraway plane, a pink ribbon in the setting sun. She mentally added it to her serial article "This is the life!" in the weekend glossy.

She was going to visit Alex the local hairdresser tomorrow, to prepare for the pregnancy shoot with "Country Sights." She had realised that she didn't need to pay £150 and a trip to London to secure beautiful highlights and she didn't seem to have the desire to visit the overcrowded noisy streets any more either.

Gervais had also finally secured a weekly article in the "Rural Gentleman," discussing what he was learning about farming. Other land owners would share their ideas and suggestions to his comments. He was gathering quite a following.

It had made him even more sure that there was a book in him. He would use all that footage he filmed across the year. The dark winter nights were ready to be filled!

Lightning Source UK Ltd.
Milton Keynes UK
UKOW07f0242280417
300101UK00009B/39/P